Bello:
hidden talent rediscovered

Bello is a digital only imprint of Pan Macmillan,
established to breathe new life into previously published,
classic books.

At Bello we believe in the timeless power of the imagination,
of good story, narrative and entertainment and we want to use
digital technology to ensure that many more readers
can enjoy these books into the future.

We publish in ebook and Print on Demand formats
to bring these wonderful books to new audiences.

www.panmacmillan.co.uk/bello

GW00535862

A. J. Cronin

Born in Cardross, Scotland, A. J. Cronin studied at the University of Glasgow. In 1916 he served as a surgeon sub-lieutenant in the Royal Navy Volunteers Reserve, and at the war's end he completed his medical studies and practiced in South Wales. He was later appointed to the Ministry of Mines, studying the medical problems of the mining industry. He moved to London and built up a successful practice in the West End. In 1931 he published his first book, *Hatter's Castle*, which was compared with the work of Dickens, Hardy and Balzac, winning him critical acclaim. Other books by A. J. Cronin include: *The Stars Look Down*, *The Citadel*, *Three Loves*, *The Green Years*, *Beyond This Place*, and *The Keys of the Kingdom*.

A. J. Cronin

LADY WITH CARNATIONS

First published in 1976 by Gollancz

This edition published 2013 by Bello
an imprint of Pan Macmillan, a division of Macmillan Publishers Limited
Pan Macmillan, 20 New Wharf Road, London N1 9RR
Basingstoke and Oxford
Associated companies throughout the world

www.panmacmillan.co.uk/bello

ISBN 978-1-4472-4395-3 EPUB
ISBN 978-1-4472-4394-6 POD

Visit **www.panmacmillan.com** to read more about all our books
and to buy them. You will also find features, author interviews and
news of any author events, and you can sign up for e-newsletters
so that you're always first to hear about our new releases.

Chapter One

That wet November afternoon it was the Holbein miniature which had drawn the dealers to Vernon's, for the sale held nothing comparable in value or importance. The miniature, sent somewhat unexpectedly from Wroxon Abbey by the Kneller family, was that known popularly as *Lady with Carnations*, a piece both exquisite and remarkable, combining in its subject—it was a tiny portait of Mlle de Quercy, daughter of the Ambassador to Henry VIII—and its date—about 1532, shortly after Holbein's return to London from Basel—the best manner and the finest period of the master.

The long gallery was crowded when at exactly half-past four the miniature came up. Bidding began, with a kind of derisive courtesy, at two thousand guineas; mounted rapidly to five thousand; stopped a moment, then rushed to seven, wavered again; then rose, with that alternate rhythm which indicates the elimination of all but two powerful competitors, to the sum of nine thousand, four hundred guineas. Here it halted.

"Nine thousand and four hundred guineas."

The auctioneer, occupying the high red rostrum with alert suavity, his hair precisely parted, his pearl pin neatly sheathed in his dark tic, rcpcatcd thc figure persuasively while his glance remained fixed on the impassively averted face of Bernard Rubin. Yet Rubin, though the bid was now against him, seemed loath to advance upon it. Eventually, however, his hooded eye, hardly visible beneath the hard rim of his bowler hat, flickered with a kind of sour perversity, and at once the auctioneer murmured:

"Nine thousand, five hundred guineas."

Immediately there came an almost imperceptible signal from the opposite side of the room.

"Nine thousand, six hundred," remarked the auctioneer blandly.

"Nine thousand, seven hundred!" Rubin went forward grimly, but again the sign came up against him.

"Nine thousand, eight hundred guineas," declared the auctioneer, and leaned again towards Rubin.

But this time Rubin had clearly finished, his limit already passed, his expression now stoically dissociated from the proceedings. If one thing had brought old Bernard Rubin up top in the antique trade, it was his faculty of knowing when to stop.

"At nine thousand, eight hundred guineas," repeated the auctioneer, his gaze sweeping the crowded room. A silence.

"For the last time, at nine thousand, eight hundred guineas." Another silence, portentous and final, terminated by the sharp tap of the hammer. "Sold at nine thousand, eight hundred guineas ... Miss Lorimer."

Katharine Lorimer rose unobtrusively from her seat at the long table and made her way towards the open double door at the end of the lofty room. Several of the dealers, stepping back politely before her passage, murmured their congratulations, but beyond a faint smile she did not seem to heed them. She would, in fact, have found it difficult to answer at that moment, for, despite the hardihood which experience had brought her, she felt her pulse throbbing painfully from the tension of those last interminable seconds. She had set her heart on the miniature, and another bid from Rubin would have beaten her.

Descending the steps, old Bernard joined her and stumped along beside her in an enigmatic silence. His car, a black-and-silver Continental model, extremely large and costly—Bernard had not failed to inform everyone of its price—stood at the kerb outside. On the doorstep Katharine and Rubin paused, met by the sound and movement of the traffic, by the brightness and the harsh mutter of London, which made the auction room seem remote and quite unreal.

"Not going my way?" Rubin asked, which was his manner of offering her a lift.

It was now nearly five, and Katharine on a sudden impulse decided not to return to business but to go home. She nodded; then, caught by a waft of rain and fog, she shivered slightly and stepped quickly into the car.

King Street was bad enough, but Piccadilly lay helpless, choked with omnibuses and taxicabs. As the car slid and stopped and slid again towards Curzon Street, Rubin's hooded eyes beneath their marked Semitic brows were fixed on Katharine with a queer ironic shrewdness.

"You gave too much, Miss Lorimer," he said at length.

"You mean too much for you, Mr Rubin?"

Rubin laughed softly. "Maybe, maybe!" he agreed with easy opulence, pausing to admire the perfect solitaire on the little finger of his left hand. "Things must be pretty good with you when you can run so high. Eh, Miss Lorimer?"

"Oh, not so bad." Katharine's tone was perfectly offhand.

"Ah, well, that's fine! That's marvellous! Especially when the rest of us in the trade are feeling things so hard. No money about, no clients, nothing doing anywhere. But you—you can up and pay ten thousand for a leetle bit of Holbein. Just like that! Why, it's almost too good to be true."

Katharine's lips parted to speak, but closed again. Instead she smiled her faint reserved smile, which seemed almost to impose a greater reticence upon her, and sat back in her corner, staring straight ahead. The decision and composure which always marked her became intensified; yet, strangely, beneath this repose there lay, it seemed, a sense of quick impulsiveness held firmly in check; and in the serious darkness of her eyes there were rich points of light which lurked and trembled on the brink of vivid life. But in the main her expression was sad, and her wide forehead bore a line, as though in the past she had known moments of great difficulty and perplexity. Her features and colouring, her brown hair and warm brown eyes in the pale oval of her face, were beautiful. Her teeth were so white that they gave freshness to even her slightest smile. She was not more than thirty-five. And yet that settled gravity, that sense of self-control, her air of contemplating some remote and abstract object, made her aloof and sometimes even formidable.

Her dress, a plain dark woollen, had clearly been chosen carelessly and in a hurry, and her hat, which sat a little back on her head, was inexpensive and did not match. It was apparent she had no interest in her clothes. But her shoes, handmade and of a fine leather, reflected just the faintest vanity in her slender, beautiful feet.

"Of course," remarked Rubin slyly, "if you cared to take a profit, say a sure ten per cent, and all nice *quick* ready cash. . ."

Katharine shook her head brusquely. "Thank you, Mr Rubin. But when I part with that Holbein, it'll be for real money."

"Real money. It don't exist any more. At least not here. No, no!" Rubin grinned, parodying a popular song. "You won't find that there here."

"Perhaps not," Katharine faced him. "Now listen, Mr Rubin, and stop cracking at me. I'm taking the miniature to New York next month. And when I get there, I'm selling it to Brandt. He's in the Argentine just now, but he'll be back on December 12th. He's buying the Holbein. He's buying it from me for twenty thousand pounds."

"Ah, Brandt—so that's the gamble," Rubin reflected with a sudden access of respect. "Well, you're a clever woman, my dear, but, on my word, if it was me, I wouldn't take the risk!"

"I can afford to take it," answered Katharine pleasantly.

"Just so." Rubin nodded like a mandarin. "Just so, my dear, you know your own position better than I do."

He darted another glance towards her, winged with inquiry and a certain unwilling regard, but the blank severity into which her features again relapsed had already dismissed the subject finally. Silence fell inside the car and continued until Rubin, as if anxious to erase an awkward impression, changed the subject.

"That little actress niece of yours, Nancy Sherwood, how's she getting along?"

Katharine turned at once, her face transformed, invested with a vivid interest. "First rate, Mr Rubin. She's just become engaged."

"Well, well. Who's the lucky man?"

Katharine's lips twitched. "I shall know to-night. I'm invited to a party—to meet him, if you please. It's really incredible the way things happen nowadays. Rather different from when I was young."

"But you *are* young, my dear," interposed Rubin deftly.

"Oh, bosh! You know what I mean. Here's Nancy goes out to Nice for a fortnight's rest before she starts in her new show and comes back trailing her future husband as if he were a new handbag."

"Well, well, things move pretty fast now," Rubin chuckled. "But it's the old ideas behind them all the time."

As the car swung into Curzon Street and came to rest opposite Katharine's flat, Rubin took one last sly thrust at her.

"Looks as if the Holbein might maybe come in handy after all!"

He patted her hand as she rose to go.

"If you don't sell it, why not give it as a wedding present?"

With the bland mockery buzzing in her ears, Katharine turned towards her apartment, one of a block of service superflats recently erected on this site. The air-conditioned luxury and almost baroque magnificence of the building were offensive to her taste, yet she found this spot convenient for her business, and it afforded her, moreover, that implacable necessity of her profession, a good address. A doorman admitted her and conducted her to the elevator, while another, equally braided, shot her to the sixth floor and obsequiously bowed her out.

Though, remembering her origins and simplicity of habit, Katharine never ceased to wonder at herself in such surroundings and often, indeed, drew a secret, childish joy from the contemplation of such diverse objects as the automatic mail chutes or the flunkies' calves, to-night her attention was otherwise engrossed. She reflected with a heavy frown on Rubin's recent remarks, asking herself how much the old fox really knew of her financial difficulties and admitting with an unconscious sigh that although he probably knew nothing, he certainly divined the worst.

The minute she was within her own door her expression relaxed further and became at once weary and harassed. She permitted herself to consider that she had had a dreadful day, with a worrying and unprofitable client at the start, hardly any lunch at the middle of it, and the mad adventure of the miniature at the end of it. Her head ached abominably, and her over driven body felt light and giddy. In one nervous gesture she tore off her hat and flung it, with her gloves and bag, upon the couch. Then she went into the little kitchenette to make some tea and, with a certain determination, to boil herself an egg.

Fifteen minutes later, as she sat at the chilly little zinc bench in the tiny pantry, confronted by the empty cup and eggshell, the absurd bathos of the thing struck her. She paid four hundred pounds a year in rental for this place alone, and another six hundred for her business premises. She had just expended ten thousand upon a miniature. And her dinner had cost approximately fourpence. She laughed until tears filled her eyes, but they were bitter tears, and had she permitted them to overflow, she must have broken down and wept.

Back in her sitting room—a quiet apartment, sparsely yet restfully furnished with a few tasteful pieces—Katharine kicked off her shoes, curled herself up in a chair, and lit a cigarette. She smoked seldom, only when she was very happy or very sad, and to-night her sense of desolation was limitless. Lately business had been damnable. The antique trade was like that; it came and went in waves. She had ridden high on the boom times like the rest of them, and now she was wallowing almost hopelessly in the slump. She was fighting, of course, and would eventually win though. Every possible economy had been effected. Though she could not escape the obligations of her leases at Curzon Street and King Street, she had laid up her car and cut her personal expenses to the bone. Yet it was hard and bitter going.

Resolutely she refused to re-examine the intricacies of her financial position. Monday would be time enough for that, when she went down again to see Mr Farrar at the bank.

Besides, to-night her melancholy was deeper and more personal.

She felt so desperately alone. She stood, in the eyes of her relatives and friends—indeed, in the eyes of the world—for that great thing, success. Her mind flashed back to her beginnings, and she saw herself at sixteen, fresh from council school and her semi-detached home in Tulse Hill, a timid little typist with Twiss and Wardrop's, Household Furnishing, Duck Court, High Holborn. She had been admitted to that gimcrack warehouse because her father knew one of the partners, a zealous Nonconformist like himself; yet she had trembled—despite the introduction—at Mr Twiss's very word, and quailed at Mr Wardrop's frown.

Life had changed for her since then. Now she was Antika of King Street, St James's, and Park Avenue, New York, famous for her taste and décor, a specialist in period reconstruction, in bijouterie and the fine arts, perhaps the best known woman antique dealer in the world. How had this happened? It had happened, she reflected sombrely, because she had willed it to happen, because she had set herself grimly to have a career, sacrificing everything fiercely, ruthlessly steeling that youthful timid heart to unbelievable hardships and effrontery. She had wanted at all costs to be *someone*. Well, it was done now. She had achieved her ambition, and oh, how hollow did she find its vanity!

The telephone at her elbow rang. With a tired reflex, since one of the complications of her life was to be perpetually at the mercy of this instrument, she reached out for the receiver.

It was her mother, ringing from Wimbledon, from the snug villa in which Katharine had installed her five years before.

"You're there, Katharine." Even over the wire old Mrs Lorimer's voice achieved the summation of tribulation and long-suffering neglect. "Well, I'm lucky this time, for a wonder. I never seem to get you these days when I ring up. You never seem to have a moment to speak to your poor old mother. Never, never!"

"Didn't I ring you last night, mother?" Katharine made the inquiry tolerantly.

"Well, what if you did?" answered the old lady peevishly. "Hello, hello! Can you hear me?"

"Yes, mother, I can hear you."

"That's right, then, don't go away. I've lots to say to you. Just wait a minute. I wrote it on a piece of paper. Now where's my glasses? Bless me, I've got them on! Now, first of all, you're coming down this week-end, aren't you, with Nancy and her new young man?"

"Yes, we're coming."

"That's right, my dear. Now listen! I want you to bring me down just a few little things: wool, sugar almonds, chocolate cake, and a nice new novel. Remember my sugar almonds especially, Katharine—you know, the kind you get me at Fortnum's. Oh, and while I think of it, you can fetch me some anchovy paste when you're in there, too. I like a little on my toast these winter evenings; somehow it makes tea so cosy by the fire. And listen, Katharine—are you listening, my dear? It's three-ply grey wool I want for my new shawl, in case I didn't mention it."

Katharine, listening patiently, now smiled faintly. "All right, mother. I'll attend to your orders."

"Orders, indeed!" Insensibly the aged voice took on an offended note. "You're blaming me for asking for a few simple necessities! Really, Katharine, how you can scold your poor old mother like that passes human understanding. If your father were alive. . ."

At the familiar invocation to the grave Katharine took a quick grip of herself. Hastily she said: "Come now, mother. You know I didn't mean anything."

A pause.

"You're not cross with me?"

"Of course not, mother."

"Well." A little sigh of appeasement came over the wire. "That's as it should be, then. Can you hear? Hello, hello, that impudent girl at the exchange is going to cut us off again. Good-night. God bless you, my dear. And don't forget my sugar almonds."

Katharine hung up the receiver with a shake of her head. Though her dear mother was more comfortable than ever she had been in her life, with her own establishment and everything she required, she had, nevertheless, a perpetual sense of being misused. She loved a grievance. Often she could be trying beyond endurance.

8

But now, with a quick glance at the clock, Katharine put her worries resolutely from her mind. She got up, went into the bathroom, and turned on the taps. Though she did not in the least feel like going out to-night, nothing in the world would make her disappoint Nancy. Quickly, carelessly, she flung off her clothes and stepped into the bath.

As she lay in the clear, unscented water, reviving under its warmth, she thought of her niece, and instinctively her frown dissolved, while her lips curved in a smile of tenderness. She adored Nancy, the daughter of her elder sister Grace, who had married Joe Sherwood against her mother's wishes, lived with him happily for fifteen years, then justified those forgotten prophecies and forebodings by dying with him instantly and ingloriously in a motor smash on the Great West Road. Ever since that tragic day Katharine had taken charge of Nancy, then a lanky girl of fourteen, lavishing every care upon her, completing her education, helping her later to study at the School of Dramatic Art, even yielding indulgently twelve months ago to her urgent wish to go on the stage. Yet, despite this record of devotion, Katharine had a sharp way with those who hinted that she spoiled her niece—nothing was too good for Nancy, the finest, dearest girl in the world.

It seemed strange to think of her as grown-up now, returning from the Riviera with this calm announcement of her engagement. And yet it was good, the best thing that could happen to her, to be settled quickly, to enjoy the best of her life with her husband and her children. That was Katharine's wish for Nancy; and to-night, for some queer reason, she wished it with her whole heart.

Rising, Katharine rubbed herself briskly with a rough towel while her fine white skin glowed respondingly. Subconsciously she could not help a thought of gratitude for her healthy body, without which she could never have withstood the burdens and buffetings of these last few years.

She dressed more slowly than usual, choosing a frock she had bought during her last visit to Paris. Ordinarily clothes were of scant importance to Katharine. She told herself bluntly she had neither cause nor time for brilliant plumage, and often indeed she went downright shabby—an attitude generally accepted with a smile as the wilfulness of a rich, successful woman. But to-night, with rising spirits, she felt she must make herself presentable for Nancy.

At half-past eight, seated before the small Vauxhall mirror on her dressing table, she was ready, and she decided, as she studied her reflection, that despite the hectic worries of the day she might pass. A few lines lay beneath her eyes, but her complexion, free of all make-up, was fresh and clear. And the fine colour of her lips, in contrast to the whiteness of her teeth, bespoke a clean and vigorous blood.

Outside, the rain had ceased, and the pavements, scoured dry by a keen wind, invited a bracing walk. On such a night Katharine liked nothing better than to step out through the quieter streets, her body inclined to meet the breeze, her cheeks tingling from her own brisk passage. But for once, respecting her evening shoes and the proprieties, she resisted the temptation. She took a taxi to the Adelphi, where, at the top of an old Adam house off John Street, Nancy had her rooms.

There was no lift in the building, which in its lower floors was given over mainly to legal offices, and as Katharine climbed the worn stone steps that circled between high stuccoed walls, the unmistakable promise of the party came towards her. Indeed, when she was admitted, passing through the hands of Nancy's own smart maid and a formal manservant evoked on such occasions, the big double room was already full of people, cigarette smoke, and noise.

The moment Katharine entered, Nancy came forward with a little outstretched sign of welcome and kissed her.

"Oh, Katharine," she said, "it's too marvellous to see you again. I've been dying to, for days."

Katharine smiled. "Then why didn't you come round? You got back on Wednesday."

"I know, darling, I wanted to most frightfully, but, oh, heavens, you don't know how rushed I've been with the new show in rehearsal, and clothes, and Chris and everything."

"I understand."

Katharine gazed affectionately at Nancy, thinking how attractive she looked to-night. Though she was only twenty-four, she had a most finished, a kind of streamlined, beauty. Her face was lovely, rather taut, with high cheekbones, slightly slanting blue eyes, and thinly pencilled brows. Her hair was lovely, too—washed to the latest blonde shade, it gleamed like spun gold. Her mouth was thin and scarlet, for upon it Nancy had not spared her lipstick. Her slender figure, under a pretence of indolence, held an odd intensity that was quite electric.

"Well," said Katharine, affecting a heavy severity, "I thought you were wedded to your art."

Nancy laughed. "I still am, darling. But that won't prevent me from marrying Chris, too."

"I see," Katharine smiled, than glanced. "Where is Chris?"

"I shall let you look for him, darling!"

"What!"

"It'll be such fun. You're always so lost among my friends, darling. I'll bet you can't find him."

"If he's a gentleman at all"—Katharine's lips twitched with amusement—"I think he ought to find me!"

At this point several people arrived with a rush, and Nancy, making a little side grimace towards Katharine, was entangled with them. Katherine walked over to the buffet and established herself strategically beside a plate of caviar canapés. She was too wise to be drawn into the centre of the party, too completely at ease to resent standing with no other company than a sandwich. Katharine's manner had that remarkable assurance derived less from the polish of many social contacts—though that was there—than from a perfect and natural simplicity. Besides, though parties amused her, Nancy's remark was accurate: she knew scarcely any of her niece's friends. One or two she did recognize: David Almoner, the young Shakespearean actor, and his wife, Nina George, the pianist; Arnold Rigby, society photographer; John Herries, director of drama at the B.B.C.; and Tony Ulrick, whose self-illustrated book of comic verse, *Libido Limericks*—which

Katharine had found nasty and effete—was enjoying just the right success. But mostly the faces were unfamiliar to her. She drank a glass of champagne and ate some more caviar. The buffet was excellent. Subconsciously she approved the fact, since in due course she would have to pay for it.

The party was intensifying now. David Chesham, author of *Moonlight in Arcady*, the play in which Nancy was to appear, came in, and a moment later Sam Bertram—the celebrated Bertie himself, than whom there was no more famous producer. Both were greeted with rapture by Nancy. Bertram waved to Katharine, an intimate, friendly gesture, indicating that he would join her presently. She gave him an answering smile. She had known Bertie for some years now, had often helped him with the décor of his shows, liked him and his blunt North Country heartiness tremendously.

The noise increased. Above it Ulrick was reciting one of his poems, while Nina George improvised a ridiculous accompaniment on the piano. Katharine had begun to get a little tired of it when suddenly she heard a voice beside her, intelligible because of its quietness coupled with a certain American penetration of tone.

"It looks as if you and I are the only sane people here."

She swung round, surprised. A tall and rather sallow man, standing carelessly with his hands in his pockets, met her inquiry with a sideways intelligent glance. He was about thirty-five, she judged, dark, thin-faced, and somewhat finely drawn; his odd longish upper lip carried a fine white scar which somehow conferred on him an air of pertinacity and coolness. Indeed, this implicit sense of self-possession backing his original remark jarred unpleasantly on Katharine.

"Must you include me?" she demanded, her brows elevated slightly.

"Well," he drawled, "I guess not, if you don't want me to."

"That would leave just you, then, as the sole representative of wise and long-suffering humanity."

He laughed silently, a quiet and unobtrusive mirth indicated only by the puckering of the skin around his eyes. "You certainly had me there, Miss Lorimer. I guess you've got even more wit than Nancy said, and she told me you had plenty."

Katharine frankly stared, and her mouth dropped open. "You don't mean that. . ."

"Sure!" He nodded and smiled, a trifle dryly. "I'm Chris Madden. Please don't look so disappointed. I know I'm not nearly good enough for Nancy, but believe me, Miss Lorimer, I'm going to try very hard."

Mechanically Katharine accepted the firm hand extended to her, while she tried to regain her composure.

"It's quite absurd of me to know so little," she said. "But I hardly expected that—that Nancy would be marrying an American."

"Why, no," he agreed in his even, reasonable voice. "And for my part, I never expected to marry an English girl."

At the thrust, which went deeper because she felt it merited, Katharine coloured, a vivid, unusual flush, and glanced at him quickly. But he was continuing, as if unconscious of her distress:

"You see, things like that don't happen the way we plan them. And when Nancy and I met in Nice—Lord, I'll never forget it—in the bright sunshine—a bit different from your fogs over here, Miss Lorimer—she sure took my breath away." He cut himself short, recaptured his reserve, and added: "Anyhow, I guess it just came over us, the way it has with people ever since Adam and Eve."

"It sounds quite idyllic."

His explanation, if indeed it were that, came so inconclusively that it made Katharine's answer uncompromising and even hostile. Perhaps she was a little jealous of Madden. She compressed her lips ever so slightly, and her gaze travelled over him again, a second and more severe inspection, noting his dress clothes, which owed nothing to Saville Row, and his linen, which was much laundered and far from smart. Her eyes narrowed. All her protective instincts towards Nancy rose up.

"And what were you doing in Nice, Mr Madden?"

"Well, it just happened I was having a vacation, the first I'd had for quite a while. I'd been in Rome and Florence and Vienna; then it struck me I'd like to see France again. I'd been there in the

War—a matter of seventeen years ago. It sounds a long time, but, gee! when I got around there, it seemed mighty short."

"Indeed!" said Katharine without enthusiasm. "Time is always deceiving. Do you plan to spend much of it here, Mr Madden?"

"That depends on Nancy, Miss Lorimer. I want us to be married pretty soon. But she's still kind of mixed up with the theatre. She's got this new play on her mind. They open in Manchester the week after next, and what with rehearsals and that, she's rather busy. It'll all pass, I guess. Anyhow, I figured on hanging around for a bit till she's through with this piece and then persuading her to come back over to America with me."

"That all seems a little sudden, don't you think, Mr Madden?" Katharine gave him a frosty smile. "We're very fond of Nancy over here. I myself am particularly attached to her. . . ."

"Oh, I know," he interrupted. "Nancy told me, Miss Lorimer. You've been simply swell to her."

"However you choose to phrase it, Nancy's happiness means everything to me. Under these circumstances it's natural I should want to know something of the man she is going to marry."

His face altered, losing its open look of animation, appearing to close up, shuttered by a mature and taciturn hardness. He turned a level glance on her and answered:

"I follow you."

There was a pause. She averted her eyes, conscious that she had wounded him by her rudeness and, paradoxically enough, upset within herself at her own intolerance. And yet, she told herself angrily, how could she be otherwise? She was cross with Nancy for having told her so little. She had expected someone quite different, someone with obvious antecedents and a definite background. This stranger, this lanky American lounging casually into her acquaintance, awoke, if not antipathy, at least a brusque suspicion which for Nancy's sake she must disprove. Silent under these thoughts, she remained standing rather unhappily beside him when Nancy approached and smiled radiantly on them both.

"I'm glad you two are on visiting terms. What do you think of him, Katharine, now you know the worst? Isn't he awful?"

Madden glanced down at Nancy, his face re-animated, suddenly alive again.

"I'm afraid she does think I'm awful. The trouble is, Nance, I didn't expect anyone so young and good-looking as Miss Lorimer, and she didn't expect anyone nearly so tough as me. I tell you, we haven't hit it off at all."

"She's very haughty," said Nancy, "but once you know her properly, she's really not too bad."

Katharine smiled constrainedly; she felt her nerves absurdly on edge.

Nancy continued: "But, seriously, Katharine darling, I want you to get to know Chris properly. You mightn't think it, but he improves on acquaintance. You'll find out when we go down to Wimbledon for the week-end."

Katharine answered with an unusual touch of sarcasm: "That's something to look forward to."

"At least you've been warned," laughed Nancy confidently. "Now, come along, both of you, and have some fun."

But Katharine, though she tried hard to lose her secret apprehension, did not have much fun. And when an hour later she left for home, she carried with her a curious feeling of uncertainty and dismay.

Chapter Two

Saturday arrived—a day of chilly winds which swept round the street corners with unexpected and intimidating violence. The weather, in fact, during these last three days had been so bad that Nancy had gone under to it with a feverish cold. In bed, her temperature two degrees over normal, she was strictly forbidden to get up. But she insisted that Madden should carry out the arrangements made for him and go, at least for one night, to Wimbledon. He could do no good in London, and in any case she would not have him hanging about her flat.

Katharine, not particularly happy at this turn of events, deferred leaving until as late as possible. It was nearly four o'clock when she rang Madden from her office and told him that she was free. He had apparently been awaiting her message, for he came almost immediately to King Street. Here Katharine occupied the first two floors of a narrow, bow-fronted building which ran back deep towards a cobbled courtyard, access to which lay through an old stone archway with carriage posts and a venerable gas lamp. It was an ideal atmosphere for a business such as hers, and she had fostered it with care. Outside the Georgian tradition had been skilfully developed. There was no display and no sign, merely a small brass plate with the name 'Antika Ltd' upon the reeded lintel; yet through the opalescent windows it was possible to discern the subdued interior of a panelled room holding many rich and mellow undertones, from the glinting patina of Queen Anne walnut to the dull lustre of an eighteenth-century brocade.

On the floor above, reached by a wide staircase with fluted balustrades and finely carved newel posts, Katharine had her office proper, a long, bright room with a large desk squat in its middle, an open fireplace, a safe in the corner, a fine Kirman carpet on the floor, and various framed schemes of décor and colour hung on the walls. Much of Katharine's business turned on the preparation of such schemes and their practical application in the restoration of old houses. She had built her unique reputation upon such expert work, and in the past her commissions, both large and profitable, had taken her inside several of the major country seats of England. She was no mere *marchande de meubles*, nor did she choose to lumber herself with a warehouse full of goods—her stock, though choice, was small. She preferred to buy selectively and only when a definite objective lay in sight. Skill, rather, was her stock in trade. It was this flair for the proper destination of an *objet d'art* which had caused her to secure the Holbein miniature with a view to steering it to the famous Brandt collection in New York.

Four o'clock struck from the lacquer bracket clock which stood upon the mantelpiece when Madden came into the office. Katharine arose at once and held out her hand. In the interval since the party she had reasoned with herself, and, driven by her inveterate sense of fairness, she had attempted to conquer her dislike of Madden and had decided to give him at least a chance.

"How is Nancy?" she asked.

"She's sort of middling," he answered. "She must stay in bed. Got fever still. She would have me come along."

Katharine nodded. "She telephoned me. I'm afraid I've kept you waiting."

"That's all right, Miss Lorimer." He gave her his unhurried smile. "I've hung around for Nancy at the theatre so much I'm getting used to waiting. It's a change for me, having time on my hands and not being tied up for every second. I guess I'll come to like it. At least, maybe."

While she pulled on her gloves, his eyes travelled over the room with calm and inoffensive appreciation.

"Nice place you have here. If it isn't raw to say it, I like your things a lot—especially that lovely carpet."

"Yes," said Katharine, and with an idea of some rudimentary explanation she continued politely: "It's eighteenth-century Persian. It probably took one man ten tears to make it. All the colours, too—they're the old vegetable dyes."

"Of course," he nodded simply. "It's a genuine Kirman-Lavehr, isn't it?"

Katharine glanced at him sharply, quite taken aback by his discernment. It bespoke keen accuracy of perception that he should place the antique rug, not only to its province, but to the actual district of its origin.

"You know about antiques, then?" she asked, gazing at him curiously.

He answered soberly. "No, honestly, I'm quite ignorant. At least judged by your standards. But I'm interested in these things, and I've tried to get wise to them. I've read a lot, and lately in Europe I've been over most of the galleries. I get quite a kick out of the things our American civilization doesn't quite cover, like Persian carpets and Italian furniture—and, oh, French salad, if you like!" He smiled. "I'm a regular old master at French salads myself."

"I see," said Katharine.

But actually she found herself more confused than ever by this new aspect of what she now admitted as an unusual and unsettling personality. All sorts of conflicting thoughts stirred within her mind, and, experiencing a certain mild exasperation, she descended the staircase with him in silence. Outside a blue landaulet stood waiting.

"I hope you've no objection," he said quickly. "Nancy told me you'd laid up your own car, so I brought this along."

"Is it yours?"

"Why no," he answered, as if surprised. "I hired it."

In spite of herself Katharine's lips drew in. "It certainly looks opulent," she murmured ironically.

She regretted the words the moment she had spoken them. But he took no notice, as if he had not heard.

The car ran smoothly, and the driver knew his way. Through St James's Park they went, past Victoria and along the embankment, where a smoky sunset threw a lovely yellow glow on the brimming river. Madden leaned a little forward in his seat, bareheaded, his soft hat crushed between his knees, absorbing the changing panorama with his eager yet collected gaze.

"This is awfully interesting to me," he remarked at length. "It's mighty different from Cleveland. I get a real kick out of it."

"You seem to get a kick, as you call it, out of a number of things, Mr Madden."

He waited before answering. "Yes, I suppose I seem pretty raw to you, but the fact is, for the last fifteen years I've been up to my neck in business with hardly a chance to breathe, let alone use my eyes. When my old man died after the War, it was pretty tough for me for a bit. And when things got going, I had to keep going with them. You don't know how a man's job can catch hold of him, Miss Lorimer, and cut out the chance to see a sunset like this and—well, if I might say it, the chance to meet a girl like Nancy."

"Perhaps I do understand." A spark of communicative sympathy awoke in Katharine, but she damped it by adding: "I hope you're not going to be disappointed in the chances of this week-end."

"Oh, no, I like meeting people. Especially Nancy's folks and," he added with simple politeness, "yours!"

Katharine smiled a trifle bleakly. "That's just where I feel I ought to warn you. You may find Mother and me extremely dull. We are very middle class, Mr Madden, and horribly suburban. Don't be misled by any glamour attaching to my work. I may meet a few important people in the way of business now and then, but don't forget that I began life as a typist at fifteen shillings a week. And I carried my lunch in a paper bag. Believe me, I'm no different now."

"No?" Turning, he made sure that she was in earnest, then he nodded his head gravely. "Well, for the first time you begin to go up in my estimation."

She could not help it; she had to laugh, for his reply got right under her dignity. "At least," she thought, "he has the saving grace of humour." And yet, at the back of her mind, she still was dubious. He saw it, too, with the extraordinary perception which stamped him, and after a moment he said quietly:

"You don't know a lot about me, do you, Miss Lorimer? I guess it worries you."

For some reason she flushed. She said sincerely: "Please don't misunderstand me. I'm not thinking of the obvious things. It's the man himself, the man who is going to marry Nancy, who matters to me."

There was silence. Oddly touched by the sympathy her words implied, he had the temptation, repressed with difficulty, to explain once and for all his position, at least to define those obvious things to which she had referred. He realized that from the outset she had completely mistaken him, an error which, from his habitual simplicity, modesty of habit, and carelessness of dress, was of frequent occurrence and which now caused him less annoyance than amusement. He hated, and had always hated, ostentation. Fashionable clothes, smart restaurants, de luxe hotels, the whole panoply and trappings of modern luxury, served merely to repel him. He had, for instance, crossed to Europe on a tramp steamer and wandered across the continent with less pretension than an ordinary tourist, putting up at out-of-the-way inns, travelling third class to mix with the people, content often to dine on a sandwich and a glass of wine.

Perhaps this asceticism derived partly from his antecedents, in particular his mother, Susan Emmet, a Vermont woman gifted with a tender, yet Spartan, sense of duty. His father, too, a Virginian, had all the candour and none of the indolence of the South. A spare, lanky, bearded man with a dry humour and a deep-set eye, Seth Madden had been a small yet sagacious trader, setting up in Cleveland as maker and retailer of a special brand of paste adhesive which he named Fixfast. The fortunes of the tiny Fixfast plant, though stable enough, had never risen high, but with the death of Seth in 1917, while Chris was in the War, they suffered a serious relapse. It was a rocky little business which young Madden took over when back in Cleveland fresh from his demobilization. Yet, bent on regeneration and expansion, he had thrown himself into work.

That was fifteen years before. How great a change those years had brought, a miracle of contrast between then and now, had to be seen to be believed. Madden never fussed or bragged, yet his quiet manner concealed a rigid strength. He brought out a new, quick-hardening, cherry gum. Its success was immediate. The business developed by leaps and bounds. He began carefully to buy in the smaller companies in the adhesive industry, together with their patents, to scrap their obsolete factories and centralize the whole in Cleveland. The parent company's capital doubled, trebled, then ran into millions. Madden was rich beyond even the wildest of his boyhood dreams. But money meant little to him except when he lavished it upon his mother, to whom he was sincerely attached. He bought her, in 1929, a small but lovely Colonial house at Graysville, her native village in Vermont.

Madden, president of International Adhesives, Inc., was one of the best known men in Cleveland. Yet his simplicity remained, and all his quiet, unassuming brevity. He was thirty-five and had worked like a slave for nearly fifteen years. Now that he was on top, he felt it time to call a halt. In the previous spring he had lifted his head from his desk and run away to Europe for a rest.

Something of this retrospect flashed through Madden's head as he sat by Katharine's side, and again he was tempted to reveal it. But he did not. And before he could change his mind they were at Beechwood, by which truly rustic name old Mrs Lorimer chose to designate her home. Already it was nearly five, and the trim outlines of the little villa were almost lost in the gathering darkness. Madden sent the car away and, carrying his own bag and Katharine's parcels, followed her up the short path between low bushes of privet into the house. They entered the drawing room, where, rocking impatiently in a chair at the fireside, sat Mrs Lorimer in person.

"What an age you've been!" she exclaimed immediately with a brisk irritation and no semblance whatsoever of a greeting. "Another minute, and the tea would have been ruined!"

She was a short, plump little woman of seventy with a restless birdlike eye and a combative set to her head. Her dress was of silk material and black, as she had not gone out of mourning for the death of her husband nine years before. Upon her hair, which was still free from grey, she wore a white lace cap, and this, added to her age, demeanour, and general appearance—in particular the tiny pouches into which her cheeks sagged—gave her a remarkable resemblance to the late Queen Victoria, a fact she did not fail to recognize and one from which she drew a secret complacent pride.

At present, however, she was not complacent but very much the martinet. Barely acknowledging Madden with a noncommittal nod, she at once attacked her daughter with a bombardment of questions relating to the execution of her commissions and to Nancy's indisposition. Only when Katharine had satisfied her did she rise and lead the way abruptly into the dining room.

Here the square mahogany table was set for an ample but extraordinary meal. It was not tea, nor supper, nor dinner, but a curious combination of all three. There was bread, both brown and white, nicely cut and buttered, cake of two kinds, a fine wedge of cheese flanked by celery, and a little silver barrel of biscuits. In the middle, under the chandelier, a blancmange shape quivered pinkly beside a crystal dish of stewed prunes. Finally, a large steaming hot fish pie was placed at the head of the table by Peggy, the diminutive maid, and behind it a majestic tea service on an enormous tray. Seating herself in state, old Mrs Lorimer poured the tea and served the pie. She took an ample helping for herself, cleverly masking it to make it seem smaller, tasted a forkful with her head critically to one side, and by a slight relaxation of her features expressed approval. Only then did she take time to look at Madden. Yet though belated, her scrutiny was sharp. And her remark was sharper.

"So you're going to marry Nancy. Well, young man, I warn you you'll have your hands full."

He answered equably: "Nancy and I will pull along all right, Mrs Lorimer."

"Maybe," declared the old lady stringently. "But it'll be a long pull and a strong pull. And heaven help you, young man, if you let go!"

This was the first of a series of remarks, proverbs, texts, and aphorisms aimed straight at Madden's head. The old lady, rigid, puritanical, and an egoist to the core, was always intimidating, but now, fortified by strong tea and the moral of her subject, she was in rampant form.

Katharine knew her mother and had learned to tolerate her most exacting moods. As she made pretence of eating the odious fish pie, which from her childhood she had loathed, she studied Madden seriously while he received her mother's fire. Frankly, his quiet good temper, or rather—she quickly corrected herself—his perfect assumption of the quality, amazed her. It was, of course, a pose, since he must be hopelessly at sea under such diverse and unknown currents of conversation and custom. Yet even so it was engaging. He listened with apparent interest, ate with apparent relish.

By the time the prunes were finally disposed of Katharine was aware that Madden, whether he wished it or not, was making a conquest of her mother. When they returned to the drawing room, where the fire had been rebanked and now cast an inviting glow on the bearskin rug, the Victorian furniture, the china and little knick-knacks on the chiffonier, Mrs Lorimer sighed contentedly.

"Sit down in that chair, Mr Madden," she indicated. "You'll find it comfortable. It was my dear husband's, and, mark you, I don't let everyone sit in it. You can look on while Katharine and I have our game of patience."

This double patience to which she referred—an unexpected concession from her Nonconformist principles—was, next to the radio, which she adored, the old lady's greatest passion.

She played it indomitably and ruthlessly with Katharine on the occasions of her week-end visits. Madden glanced interrogatively at Katharine, and perhaps he read her face, for he said persuasively:

"Your daughter looks awfully tired, Mrs Lorimer. How about a little game with me?"

"Humph! Katharine's usually tired when it comes to doing something for her old mother."

"No, but I'd like a game," Madden said. "And let me tell you I'm pretty smart at it."

"Oh, you are?" said Mrs Lorimer, scenting battle. "Smart, indeed!

I like that! Well, come away, and I'll give you a pretty smart beating." She glanced at the clock. "We've got a good half hour. There's a splendid play on the wireless at eight—*The Black Pearl*. We must listen to that!"

They sat down to the game at the green baize table before the fire while Katharine, glad of the respite, installed herself in the sofa and watched with a sense of rising expectation. She knew from long experience that unless Madden's individuality were wholly negative, trouble, serious trouble, must ensue.

Mrs Lorimer began well. She won the cut and dealt good cards, her spectacles nicely settled and her bag of sugar almonds conveniently by her side. She made an excellent run and sat back with a satisfied sigh while Madden discarded only a few cards, then failed. Mrs Lorimer got in again with another long run, and for a while her good fortune continued. Then, unexpectedly, the luck changed, and Madden, playing confidently, commenced a series of runs which placed him well in the lead.

At this point, as Katharine had anticipated, her mother began to cheat. The old lady had in fact this one frightful foible. She could not endure to be beaten. Never, never. Come what may and at all costs, she must win. Whether or not it was the blind spot on her conscience made no odds; the fact remained that rather than suffer the ignominy of defeat she would cheat flagrantly, mercilessly.

Madden, of course, saw the cheating at once, and Katharine, her dark eyes on the players, awaited the dénouement. If he protested, there would be a scene; if he said nothing, he would be a humbug. But Madden, it seemed, was steering a different course. With a solemn face he began to aid the old lady in her cheating, subtly at first, then with increasing intention, giving her back good cards instead of bad, failing stupidly to take his turn, and generally inciting her to greater, and still greater, fraud. At first Mrs Lorimer chuckled and took the gifts which the gods were offering, but gradually her expression changed. She darted one or two doubtful glances at him, then suddenly when within an ace of winning, she hesitated, faltered, and blushed.

"Why do you look at me like that?" she demanded hotly.

"Gee, Mrs Lorimer," he answered gravely, "I was just admiring the way you play. I've been all over the States and Europe and the rest of it, and I never saw playing like that anywhere before."

"What!" she ejaculated.

"No, ma'am." His voice took on a Southern drawl. "That's the best sure-fire card playin' I ever saw in all my born days."

Her bright eyes nearly popped from her head. She took a long, pugnacious breath and drew herself up, ready to destroy him. And then, all at once, she began to laugh. She laughed unrestrainedly, scattering the cards, upsetting her almonds; Katharine had never seen her laugh like that before.

"Oh dear, oh dear," she gasped at last. "That's the funniest thing. The best card playing—did you hear him, Katharine?—in all his born days."

"Why, certainly, ma'am," he went on. "I sure. . . ."

But, rocking helplessly, tears of merriment running down her cheeks, she stopped him with one weak hand. "Don't," she wheezed, "you'll be the death of me. My dear young man, it's too funny. The *best* card playing—and me cheating you all the time!"

It was a grand joke, perhaps the best ever heard in the stuffy little room. But when it ended, the old lady recollected herself with a start.

"My goodness!" she declared, wiping her eyes and peering suddenly at the clock. "If we're not missing the play on the wireless!" And, more spryly than one would have believed, she went over to the radio and switched it on.

A moment's hesitation, then the instrument buzzed to life. True enough, the play had begun. A girl was speaking.

Madden looked at Katharine sharply, to find that Katharine was staring at him. In a moment, too, old Mrs Lorimer's eyes widened, darted from one to the other. The girl went on speaking.

"It can't be," said Madden suddenly.

No! Surely it could not be. Nancy was in bed with a temperature. Nancy hadn't said a word about this. Nancy was ill, unable to get up.

"Well, I declare!" exclaimed the old lady in genuine wonderment.

"There must be some mistake," said Katharine in a bewildered tone.

But there was no mistake. The voice coming so plainly over the air was Nancy's voice.

Chapter Three

All that day Nancy had remained in bed, her head throbbing, her limbs weighed down by an influenzal ache. She loathed being laid up, and that made her more restless still. Though she was not seriously concerned over *Moonshine in Arcady*, since the play was well advanced and no rehearsal had been called for over the week-end, her nature resented even this temporary interference with her nicely ordered little life. Nancy, indeed, had a disconcerting veneer of egoism which sometimes inclined her towards petulance when things did not go all her own way. Perhaps, in spite of Katharine's disclaimer, the affection which had been lavished upon her had slightly spoiled Nancy. She took so many things for granted. Someone, explaining this idiosyncrasy, had said of Nancy that she had still to grow up.

To-day, however, she would have protested that she had been irreproachable in her behaviour. She had taken her quinine faithfully every four hours and submitted to the diet, restricted to hot fluids, with which Mrs Baxter, her daily maid, had steamingly supplied her, During the forenoon, propped up on her pillows, she wrote a few letters that had long been outstanding. This duty done, she let her thoughts dwell pleasantly on Madden until she fell asleep for about an hour. Afterward she took up a book from beside her bed and tried to keep her mind on it.

The book that Nancy held was unexpected in the hands of so ingenuous an invalid, who might reasonably have sought distraction in a swift detective tale or the mild vacuity of a light novelette. For it was the plays of William Shakespeare. A glance at the adjoining bookshelves was even more illuminating. These were filled almost entirely with plays, at least with those plays which might be accounted classic: Marlowe, Congreve, Ibsen, Molière, Sheridan, Shaw—all were there. And in addition there were interspersed various biographies of famous personalities of the drama. It was an amazing library for a frivolous young actress of the modern stage.

Yet a glance round Nancy's bedroom would have induced an even greater perplexity. There were none of the expected fripperies. No exotic telephone covers or overdressed dolls. The room was austere as a monastic cell and as rigorously ordered. Only two photographs stood upon the chest of drawers—one of Madden and the other of Katharine—while on the walls, which were simply painted white, there hung a single picture, a large and beautiful drawing of the famous Eleonora Duse. This portrait of one of the greatest actresses the world has ever known undoubtedly contained the clue which solved the puzzle of Nancy's room and the even greater enigma of Nancy herself.

Down in her secret heart Nancy was mad about the theatre. Not the ordinary stage-struck madness, but a deep and burning adour to express herself through the vivid, pulsing art of mime. Whence it came Nancy could not guess, unless some ancestor of her happy-go-lucky father had passed this eager heritage to her blood. But there it was, dating back even to her earliest days.

Unhappily for Nancy and this fervour which possessed her, she could not imprint it with a due solemnity. A few of her intimate friends truly recognized her ambition and the intensity of her application to her dramatic studies, though whether they believed she would ultimately succeed was quite a different matter. But the important people, Katharine, for instance, and now Madden, were merely inclined to smile at Nancy's soul-disturbing aspirations. They could not, or would not, take her seriously.

For this, in a sense, Nancy had herself to blame. She was extremely young, with all the uncertainties and mannerisms of adolescence. Her moods, in which she could manifest both pique and caprice, did not predispose one towards belief in the constancy of her ideals.

She had, too, a habit of flippancy, and in conversation used the current coin, which was often cheap, of the modern smart set. She was, in a word, a complex little person, like a seesaw, now up, now down, and it was difficult to determine in which of these positions she would ultimately finish.

Such an analysis of Nancy's character, had it been presented to her, would have disturbed her profoundly, for she was at heart both sensitive and sincere. However, no one had done this for her up to date. Nor was she likely at this moment to pursue the examination for herself. She was too busy with her Shakespeare, immersed, for all her throbbing temples, in the study of *King Lear*. She saw herself as Goneril first, then Regan, and finally the slim Cordelia.

Finished at last, Nancy laid down the book. She felt tired. Time passed. The afternoon merged into evening. Her daily woman took her departure, promising to look in again at nine that night to see that she was comfortable. Nancy dozed a little, her reverie again of Madden, off-setting her present malaise by the happy prospects of the future. And then, cutting across the web of her abstraction, came the ringing of the telephone.

Nancy picked up the receiver and recognized the voice as John Herries' before he had time to announce himself. She had a particular aptitude for voices. And Herries, from his tone, was plainly relieved to have made contact with her.

"Look, Nancy," he declared somewhat urgently, "I'm frightfully glad I've got hold of you. Yes, I am at the B.B.C. And I'm in the most awful fix. You know we're on the air to-night with *The Black Pearl*. It's a definitely important show, eight o'clock, peak hour, and all that. Well, listen, Nancy! Sylvia Burke has gone back on me. She's sick. Think of it. My lead goes down at four hours' notice. That's why I want you, Nancy. I want you to pick up the part. Now hurry over, there's a good girl. And we'll run through the script together."

"But, John," protested Nancy, "I—I don't know that I can come!"

"What! Are you out of your senses! Don't you realize this is jam for you? Deputizing for Sylvia Burke. And a couple of million listening in."

Nancy pressed her hand rather dizzily against her hot head. What Herries said was absolutely true. Sylvia Burke was perhaps the most important comedy actress of the day. It was a miraculous chance to advance her own reputation, to exhibit her name before that enormous public who would be tuning in to hear the star.

"What's wrong with Sylvia?" she temporized feebly.

"Influenzal cold," snapped Herries. "Temperature a hundred degrees. They absolutely won't let her move."

At any other moment Nancy would have laughed.

"You're not worried about the script?" persisted Herries. "Just a matter of reading it through."

"No, no, I'm not worried about that," answered Nancy, reaching for the clinical thermometer beside her bed. "Just hang on a minute, please."

She slipped the thermometer under her tongue and left it there for sixty agonizing seconds. Then she looked. The reading was a hundred and one degrees. Her heart sank dully. She couldn't go. It was impossible. She must not take such a risk. The thing was sheer insanity.

"Well?" broke in Herries almost with exasperation. "Have I got to stay here all night? What's wrong with you, Nancy? I thought you had your head screwed on the right way. Are you coming or are you not?'

Nancy's lips opened to say: "No," when all at once her eye lit on her portrait of Duse that hung, like an inspiration, on the wall in front of her. Duse, her ideal, the great Duse, who had once played half-crazy with *tic douloureux* rather than disappoint her public. Something leaped in Nancy's throat; an inspiration, a quick surge of courage.

"Of course I'm coming, John," she found herself saying. "I don't feel so good as I might. But I'll be with you in half an hour."

She clicked the receiver down on his burst of gratitude. She was quite out of her mind. She would get frightfully ill, catch some dreadful complication if she went to-night. Katharine would be terribly upset with her, and Chris—well, hadn't she said she was too ill to go with him to Wimbledon? A pang shot through her, but passed as quickly. Chris loved her. He would not be cross with her. He would understand.

Summoning all her resolution, Nancy got up. She felt extremely shaky, but with an effort she managed to dress. She put on her heaviest clothes, her fur coat, and as an after-thought wrapped a thick scarf round her neck. She took a big dose of her medicine and rang for a taxi. Then, staring at herself in the glass, she shook her head slowly, made a melodramatic little gesture, and switched out the light.

Chapter Four

There ought, of course, to have been a sensation, a real, authentic *frisson*. Nancy should have fainted at the microphone to the consternation of the million fans or else, returning from the studio in a snowstorm, have contracted double pneumonia and passed away to the wailing of violins some twenty-four hours later.

As it was, she gave a competent performance—considering the shortness of the notice and the muddled condition of her head—and came back to the flat to a barrage of reproaches from Beechwood. Madden was already in the car on his way to her.

Next morning there were no headlines. Against the accepted formula for tragedy, Nancy was better, much better. Her temperature actually was normal, and on Monday she was fit to return, with just one sheepish glance at the picture of Duse, to the rehearsals of *Moonlight in Arcady*.

Meanwhile Katharine also was back at work. She sat in her office with her chin propped reflectively on her palms, while before her, on the desk, in its case of dark green velvet, lay the Holbein miniature which Mr Sugden, one of the partners in Vernon's, had delivered to her in person that morning. Katharine's eyes dwelt on the miniature with a dark, intensive scrutiny.

It was a lovely thing, rich with a delicate and sombre art. The woman, Lucie de Quercy, stood at a double-tiered table which carried, above, a strip of red brocade and, below, a mandolin and some open books. Her dress was of dark maroon trimmed with ermine, and in her hand, resting lightly on the brocade, she carried a spray of white carnations. She was beautiful, with a secret, an almost enigmatic, beauty—pale, slender, wise. Her eyes especially, of a deep and luminous brown, seemed to hold an infinite understanding, and to gaze up into Katharine's as if they were alive. So intimate, so confiding, were those eyes that they became fraught with meaning, bearing a message for Katharine, drawing her gently backward through the dim arches of the years into the far, incalculable past. Fascinated, Katharine found herself returning the gaze of Lucie de Quercy, yielding to the influence of that sweet yet pensive personality.

The story of Lucie, inseparable from the miniature and a matter of open history, was well known to Katharine. The young Frenchwoman had come from Paris with her father, Comte de Quercy, to the court of Henry VIII, partly to attend the court but mainly to sit for her portrait to Holbein, who had then returned from Switzerland after severe financial reverses, and settled in London. Behind her Lucie left her betrothed, Pierre de Noailles. Theirs was no formal affection but the flowering of a rare love. The portrait was painted—the same that now hangs in the royal picture gallery at The Hague.

And then, as an afterthought, Lucie begged Holbein for the miniature, intending it as a gift for de Noailles. It was done, more exquisite even than the major work, and in the spring of that year Lucie returned with the Comte to Paris.

They were met in France by the news of the death of de Noailles, killed in a duel two days before. Lucie's miniature became no more than a tragic memento of her loss. She never married. Broken-hearted, she accepted her destiny. Devoting her life to good works, she died at the age of thirty-seven in a convent.

A knock on the door recalled Katharine abruptly to the present. She sat for a moment without moving, then with a little shiver called: "Come in!"

Mr Walters, her head man, entered. He stood by the desk, a long brown package in his hands, gazing over her shoulder at the miniature. "Very nice, Miss Lorimer," he said at length in his subdued, respectful tone. "Very nice indeed."

Mr Walters was always respectful and always dignified. A fatherly gentleman of sixty, refined and neat in his attire, with a high, stiff collar and near-clerical suit, he looked like a churchwarden of a High Episcopal church. Even his walk was reverent, each step a gentle pressure on the carpet. He had been with Katharine now for many years, and she knew by heart his foibles and weaknesses, which included an insatiable predilection for strong tea and the Gothic Period. He was so sound and stable he seemed an institution in himself, and his devotion to the antique profession, as opposed to the horrid brutality of trade, was most impressive. It amused Katharine occasionally to shock him by shouting for him from the head of the staircase: "Forward, Mr Walters, please!" But in the main she duly treasured him.

"A little masterpiece," went on Mr Walters admiringly. "It's remarkable, isn't it, how the detail does not impair the decorative effect."

"Very remarkable," said Katharine dryly.

"And so typical of Holbein, poor man. Hmm! Strange I should say 'poor man'. I always think of him with sympathy, though, dying of the plague the way he did. Fifteen forty-three, wasn't it? Mm, yes. He was only forty-six. He had such a shocking time in Basel, too, before that, losing all his money. Still, he must have enjoyed painting this. She's a lovely woman. Do you know, Miss Lorimer, forgive me for passing the remark, but she's a little like you!"

"Nonsense!"

"Oh, but yes, Miss Lorimer, if I might venture to contradict. I see a distinct resemblance. The eyes there, exactly like yours." He paused. "I presume you know her history."

"Yes, yes," Katharine said brusquely. "Every collector knows it. Don't let's rake it up again. Poor thing!"

Her tone took him rather by surprise.

"Of course not, Miss Lorimer. I merely thought it might be interesting. . . ."

Katharine turned with a forced smile. "It'll be a lot more interesting when we sell the miniature. We need the money, Walters. And you know it. Tell me, has anything come in about that Ansen commission?"

"Yes, Miss Lorimer." Walters hesitated. "Lady Ansen rang up

this morning." His voice expressed a pained concern. "She's decided to leave over the renovations."

"What!" Katharine's eyes sparkled with sudden anger. "But she told us on Friday we could go ahead."

"I know, Miss Lorimer." Walters' head drooped. "She's gone back on that. She—she said things were rather difficult at present."

"Difficult!" Katharine echoed the word mirthlessly. With a great effort she conquered her indignation. She had a pretty temper on occasion, but there was little point in venting it now.

"I'm sorry, Miss Lorimer," Walters was saying. "I did my best to persuade her."

"I know, I know. And of course it isn't your fault, Walters. I'm not blaming you. Lady Ansen was right. Things *are* difficult. Difficult for everybody. Difficult for us!" Katharine sighed, and her eyes reverted to the miniature. "We've got to put this Holbein over pretty successfully, and pretty soon."

"You mean Mr Brandt, Miss Lorimer?"

"Yes, Brandt. He'll want it for his collection. I know he will. If he hadn't been down in Argentina, he'd never have missed it at the sale. He'd have bid up to twenty thousand for this, Walters. And that's the price I'm going to ask him now."

"Yes, Miss Lorimer." Walters' voice was hushed. "You did well with Mr Brandt over those porcelains. A nice gentleman. Excellent taste. And so wealthy."

"Yes! He's wealthy!" Katharine answered grimly.

"You'll go over yourself, Miss Lorimer?"

"Yes, I'll go over. Look up the sailings for the beginning of next month. I think the *Pindaric* goes about the seventh. She's a good ship. And what's more important, Walters, they'll give me a nice cabin at the minimum rates."

Walters' eyes sought the floor again. "Is it as bad as that, Miss Lorimer? I thought—why, of course I *knew*—but I didn't quite realize. ...." He paused, then with embarrassing dramatic effect drew himself up. "If there's anything I can do, Miss Lorimer—in the way of a cut, perhaps—or anything to help you. . ."

Katharine's expression lightened. She smiled—genuinely,

affectionately. "It only wanted that, Walters! White-haired retainer offers life savings to prevent foreclosure of the mortgage. No, no, it's not so bad as that! We've been up against it before. We'll pull through this time again. Now don't stand there gaping as if the bailiffs were downstairs. Off you go and get some work done."

"Yes, Miss Lorimer," stammered Walters, retreating. He was almost gone when he remembered the package in his hand. "Oh, I forgot, Miss Lorimer. This came for you."

He came back, placed it upon the desk, turned, and tiptoed reverently away. The door closed behind him without a sound.

Free of the necessity of pretence—she could never have met Walters with the full gravity of her position—Katharine allowed her expression to lapse into sadness again. Almost with apathy she approached the package. She was some time occupied with the knots, since she could never bear ruthlessly to cut string, especially such handsome tricolour twine as this; but at last it was untied and the lid removed. Then her eyes widened, and a real delight rushed into them. The box was full of lovely double carnations. Almost before she saw the card she knew that they were from Madden, for she remembered having mentioned on their drive to Beechwood, commenting on a garden they had passed, that these were her favourite flowers. She picked up his card—a plain one, she noted—her eyes dwelling upon the neat lettering,

Chris Madden
Cleveland   Ohio

before passing to the message below.

"In gratitude for an interrupted week-end—and Nancy," he had written.

She could not repress a throb of amusement at his cool assumption of proprietary rights over her niece. Yet it was pleasant to have these lovely blooms; no one had sent her flowers for ages, and that they should be her favourites—it was clever of him to have remembered her stray remark. As she placed them in an old Worcester bowl whose dull gold and brown offset their lovely texture, she thought with an inward smile, "I mustn't let him get round me this way."

A rich fragrance filled her room when she had placed the bowl to her liking on the desk. Gratified, she took the miniature and locked it in her safe. Then she turned and, her features altering, addressed herself to the painful matter of business. She took a pencil and began to figure out her liabilities on a pad.

It was true that she had paid ten thousand for the miniature, yet she had done this almost entirely with borrowed money; her cash in hand had been no more than four thousand, but she had long been known to the City and Southern Counties Bank; and Mr Farrar, of the St James's Branch, straining friendship and credit to the limit, had loaned her the additional six thousand pounds on the stock and good will of her business. Actually the loan had been issued on her record of integrity rather than on her assets.

So far she stood exactly clear, but the demands falling on her at the beginning of the year were too formidable to to contemplate. Rent and rates; tax and super-tax, bitter reminder of her good years to the tune of two thousand pounds; bills due for fabrics, materials, and other goods added another eight hundred to the score. But there was no need of further detail; already the figure was known to her. The liabilities she must meet in January totalled approximately five thousand pounds. It was this ominous and unalterable fact which had forced her into the desperate adventure of the miniature. And now, with a sudden quickening of her intention, she saw the vital necessity of carrying it to a successful conclusion. Then everything would be well. She could meet her obligations, pay off the bank overdraft, start again with a comfortable balance and the prospect of better times to come. She must sell the miniature, she must, she must!

This conclusion reached, she gazed at her figures with a certain fixity, then, squaring her elbows, she set to work on a letter to Breuget, her manager in New York, telling him when to expect her and how to establish preliminary contact with Brandt. It was an important letter, and though the tapping of Miss Mills's typewriter was now significantly silent, Katharine wrote it herself in the thin, clear hand which somehow characterized her.

She had just finished when a knock came on the door and Miss Mills appeared in person. On her prim bespectacled face she wore, despite her efforts to subdue it, an arch, incongruous smile which immediately advised Katharine of its cause.

"It's Mr Upton," murmured Miss Mills. "He says he has an appointment with you, Miss Lorimer."

"For lunch, I suppose?"

"Why, I suppose so, Miss Lorimer."

Katharine observed the blushing Mills with a queer introspection. Charley Upton was devastating, no doubt, but it was his effect on the spinsterish Miss Mills, this remote yet truly feminine flutter which his advent always induced in her, that somehow struck at Katharine and depressed her. A man, she reflected despondently, still meant something in the narrow, desiccated life of our Miss Mills.

"Very well, then," she nodded. "You'd better let him in."

A moment later Charley Upton came in.

"You know, Charley," said Katharine before he could speak, and she had to be quick to anticipate him, "some day I'm going to make you take Miss Mills out to lunch. She'd probably die of heart failure. But I daresay she'd think it would be worth it."

Charley Upton smiled a nice easy smile that went with the gardenia in his buttonhole. "The Mills of God type slowly," he remarked airily, "but they type exceedingly well! She's not a bad old thing by the look of her."

"Heavens!" exclaimed Katharine. "She's not old. She's just choked up with business and her wretched women's club and milk and buns and running for the tube and buying herself a new hot-water bottle. If it wasn't for her weekly dose of the cinema and Clark Gable, and you, Charley, she'd probably pass out altogether. She's the classic example of the female wage earner, the businesswoman, Charley. I tell you, and I ought to know."

Charley laughed. "You seem to be arguing my way to-day. Usually you're so full of Big Business I can't get a word in edgeways."

Katharine gazed at him as he stood there, looking exactly what he was, an easy-going, good-natured fellow, not over-blessed with brains, a trifle over-groomed and a little overdressed, but on the whole likeable and genuine. The manifest advantage of Charley was that he never pretended to be what he was not, never insisted that the vacuum was full. He was forty-five, though he seemed younger, and had never done a hand's turn in his life. His father had started life in a Birmingham solicitor's office, worked his way through college, taken his law degree, established himself in practice, and risen by swift strategic steps to part proprietorship of a small provincial newspaper which for five years he controlled. Concentrating his ambitions on the Press, he expanded, amalgamated, sold out, then bought in again in London. His success continued until finally he stood as sole proprietor of the *Sunday Searchlight*, that incredibly popular Sunday newspaper with a penchant for the police and the divorce courts and a circulation of five million and a half.

On the old man's death Charley found he was worth more than he could ever hope to spend, and his capacities in that direction were not slight. He had a seat on the board of directors of the paper which he seldom occupied, though at the Annual Banquet and the Staff Ball he was invariably the leading figure. For the rest, he did nothing. Yet he did it elegantly. He belonged to half a dozen clubs and had scores of friends, hunted a little and shot a little, enjoyed his dinner and a good story after it, slapped a great many good fellows on the back, kept himself fit, spent hours with his tailor, shirtmaker, and bootmaker, and whole afternoons in the Turkish baths, lent money to everybody, yet was nobody's fool. In short, that phrase so often given to a very pleasant, well-mannered, yet slightly dull horse was very applicable to Charley—there was not an ounce of vice in him.

Eight years before, he had met Katharine Lorimer at a Charity Ball and, in his own classic phrase, been struck absolutely of a heap. He proposed the following week, and since then he had at intervals forced upon Katharine the distressing necessity of again refusing him. Between whiles, of course, Charley had some consolation from the ladies of the chorus, but these were empty little episodes, and, to his credit, Charley never hid them. Among such affairs his devotion to Katharine bloomed like a splendid flower in a rather shabby garden. There was such a faithful quality in Charley's affection, and he had still such an eager hope of ultimate success, that it was impossible not to hate hurting him.

Lately, indeed, Katharine had felt a strange fear of herself. She did not love Charley, and she had definitely renounced the idea of marriage at the outset of her career. But at the back of her head lay an unformed notion that his fondness for her, allied to the immense solidity of his position, might one day drive her into some manifestation of weakness—an appeal for help, maybe, or even what was psychologically subtler and much more likely to occur, that she should mentally adopt him as a refuge, a safeguard from the harassing demands of her life. That she, Katharine Lorimer, who had so sternly moulded her own career, should come to acknowledge such a primitive and absurd necessity as the dominance of a man intellectually her inferior was, and could be, no more than an upsetting nightmare. Yet she had her moments of nervousness over it, especially when Charley sat near her, or took her hand. They made her draw down her brows when she looked at him, a trifle forbiddingly. And it was in this fashion that she observed him now.

"You haven't explained yet," she declared, "what you mean, coming bothering me at this time of day."

"It's the right time of day. I've come to take you to lunch."

She made a firm gesture of negation with her head. "I'm too busy."

"You're always too busy, Katharine. But you're coming."

"No, I'm not coming."

"Oh, yes, you are. I've booked a table at the Embassy."

"Now, listen, Charley," she remonstrated sternly. "I've told you before I've my work to do. How do you expect me to make an honest living if you come disturbing me like this?"

He laughed easily. "You don't have to make an honest living. You're the most prosperous woman in the West End of London. You're in all the papers with that Holbein thing."

"Don't tell me I'm in the *Sunday Searchlight*!"

"Not yet, but you will be. But to get back to the point, I've ordered the lunch."

"What have you ordered?"

"I ought to know by this time what you like for luncheon. Sole a la bonne femme, Florida salad, and cheese soufflé."

She could not help it. Despite herself her lips twitched, and her frown dissolved. She jumped up companionably. "I'll come, then," she declared, "but I've got to be back here at this desk in one hour. Understand. At two p.m. sharp! And I'm coming only because of the soufflé, *not* because of you."

Charley laughed again, watching her jam on her hat and fling a short fur cape over her shoulders.

"So long as you come!" As he followed her downstairs he added: "And by the by, after the cheese soufflé, Katharine, I've something to ask you. You see, it's high time I proposed to you again."

Chapter Five

On Saturday, the last day of November, Nancy left for Manchester with the rest of the *Moonlight in Arcady* company, and Madden accompanied the party as arranged. They were opening on the following Monday at the Royal Theatre, and since any one of Chesham's plays made first-rate news, they had quite a spectacular send-off from St Pancras. Nancy was in the gayest spirits. She had armfuls of flowers, a middle place in two of the group flashes, and another with David Chesham himself. Katharine, aware of Nancy's liking for a little publicity, had arranged for this beforehand with the agencies.

Madden, she had to admit, behaved well, keeping himself near yet unobtrusive, and attentive to Nancy in that practical undemonstrative style so particularly his own. Katharine had time only for a word with him before the train pulled out, a rather conventional admonition that he take care of Nancy, yet she went home feeling herself more favourably disposed towards him than ever.

On Tuesday morning she turned eagerly to the papers. As was to be expected, there was not much in the London press, though the majority of the paragraphs were favourable to the new play. But the Manchester dailies had each a full report, and the general tone was politely laudatory. With a throb of pride Katharine came across a notice which praised Nancy's performance. Katharine herself, having seen Nancy in everything which she had hitherto done, had no doubt about her talent. She was extremely good. It was particularly in her delineations of the modern young woman that she excelled, for she could produce without effort a hard brilliance, a tired and youthful indifference to the contemporary scene, which combined both accuracy and irony and so became not only a portrait but a satire.

For all her pride and genuine delight in Nancy's rapid progress on the stage, Katharine had still an attitude of mild indulgence towards it. She could not bring herself to be serious when Nancy, with genuine intensity, spoke of her profession and her devotion to the drama. The drama, thought Katharine with an inward smile, was such a wide, uncertain quantity, while Nancy was so slight and pretty, and poised so urgently for happiness, that the correlation of the two seemed quite incongruous. Nevertheless, this did not prevent Katharine from rejoicing in Nancy's present success. She hoped the piece might have a long run when it came to the West End. This, at least, she reflected, would give the Madden situation time to resolve itself.

During the next two days Katharine was busy with the preliminaries of her departure, and her head was full of affairs more pressing than the play. But on Friday she had a most unexpected reminder. Just after noon the telephone rang, and Madden's voice struck upon her ear.

"Are you still up north?" she demanded when her first sharp surprise subsided.

"No," he answered. "I'm at my hotel here. I had to come back to London yesterday. Urgent business. It was a tough break, but I had to make it."

"How is the play going?"

"Oh, fine, fine," he answered, perhaps a shade too quickly. "Nancy is an absolute knockout. I want to tell you all about it. Say, Miss Lorimer, will you come to lunch?"

Katharine reflected. She was free of engagements. Yet she had no desire to be under obligation to Madden. She said:

"No! You come to lunch with me."

"All right." He accepted without demur. "Pick me up here. Only let's go somewhere quiet. Suppose we go to one of those Fleet Street chophouses I've heard so much about."

About an hour later Katharine, having acceded to his request, sat opposite Madden in one of the stalls of the Cheshire Cheese, surrounded by a cheerful bustle of hospitality and hearing his account of the northern trip. He spoke warmly. The opening had gone well, they were playing to fair houses, and Nancy in particular had been grand. Yet Katharine, listening without comment, her eyes fixed on his dark, mobile face, read a hesitancy between his words and a refusal to commit himself fully.

"They're tightening up some of the scenes," he concluded. "And changing the end of the second act. That ought to improve it when it comes up here."

"You don't think much of it," said Katharine bluntly.

"Well, no," he admitted candidly. "It isn't nearly good enough for Nancy!"

Though he did not know it and Katharine herself made no sign, it was the most telling answer he could have given. Spoken with ingenuous simplicity, it went straight to Katharine's heart and swept the last of her prejudice away. She decided at that moment that she liked Madden and henceforth would accept him without reserve.

"You're very much in love with Nancy, aren't you?" she asked.

"I certainly am, Miss Lorimer," he answered steadily. "And that's why I want to talk to you to-day."

There was a pause, then she said, crumbling her roll into tiny fragments: "I daresay you've found me pretty tiresome. I might even have said suspicious. But then, I'm fond of Nancy, too—terribly fond of her. She means really everything in the world to me." She looked up quickly, almost apologetically, a faint colour in her cheeks. "Sorry to be so sentimental and old-fashioned, but I'm only trying to explain my attitude. I do so want Nancy to be happy, and in spite of all this horrible modern cynicism I know the only way she will be happy is by marrying the right man, the man who loves her, who'll take her away from this silly business of the stage and make a real home and—oh dear, oh dear," she broke off self-consciously, "there I go again. But I can't help it. Out of date or not, it's exactly how I feel about Nancy."

"Believe me," he replied very seriously, "that's the very thing I had to say to you. Yes, I'm darn glad you do feel that way, for it's just how I feel myself. Nancy's a swell little actress, but—well, I hate seeing her fooling around in these stupid plays and doing stunts like she did at the B.B.C. So far as I'm concerned, it's just a waste of time. Oh, I know she wants to play Shakespeare. But doesn't every young actress? And honestly, when she marries me, though I guess I'm no Romeo, I'd rather she played Juliet back home."

She smiled at the turn of phrase which epitomized all she might have struggled to say. "Then we do understand each other. We're friends. And you go right ahead with Nancy."

"That's a real break for me, Miss Lorimer. And while we're about if, if you don't object, I think I'd better make it Katharine."

"You make it anything you like. So long as you don't blame me for being such a dragon."

"If you're a dragon," he drawled, "I guess you're the nicest one I ever saw."

They both laughed, and the tension which had grown insensibly during those last few moments suddenly relaxed. A silence followed. Madden, as though sensible that enough had been said on a difficult subject, made no effort to pursue it. Instead he looked around the old room, on whose time-darkened walls hung many relics of the past.

"I've always wanted to come here," he remarked. "I suppose that sounds very banal and American to you. But it's true. It'll always give me a real kick to think I've lunched at the Cheshire Cheese."

"The food *is* good," she agreed.

He smiled. "Oh, you know it isn't that, Miss Lorimer—sorry, I mean Katharine. Of course this pie is marvellous; but I'm thinking of Dr Johnson and Boswell and Goldsmith. How they came here and talked and wrote and had their ale under these old rafters. And nothing changed, either. The waiters still running about in aprons and bawling through the hatch like the stagecoach had just come in. Oh, I daresay that's raw stuff—naïve, I suppose you'd call it—but I love these old things, and I guess I'll never have enough of them."

His enthusiasm was infectious. She said:

"There's lots to see in London if you're interested."

He nodded and helped himself to celery from the old glass dish that stood on the checkered tablecloth. "Yes, I know. I've been too busy with Nancy to have much opportunity. I wouldn't expect her to come trailing through museums." He smiled again, then was serious. "But I guess I'll have a look around this afternoon. There's plenty I want to see right here in the City if I can find it."

He was so genuine in his intention that Katharine's heart warmed to him. She reflected that he probably did not know a soul in London beyond herself, and she had a swift vision of him asking his way of policemen and getting lost rather disconsolately in the gathering gloom of the Inns of Court. She exclaimed on an impulse:

"Suppose you let me show you round. I ought to know my way about if anyone does."

His face lighted up in a manner which was extraordinarily attractive. "Oh, would you? But it would bore you. And you've far too much to do."

"I think I can find time." Her lips compressed themselves on a smile. "And it mightn't bore me as much as you think."

It was half-past two when they went out into Fleet Street and, with the cupola of St Paul's standing proudly in the sky above them, walked up towards the Strand. Katharine had not been in this part of the City for years, and it gave her, as she had half-anticipated in her remark to Madden, an extraordinary thrill to walk those pavements which had known the hurrying footsteps of her youth. As they passed outside the Law Courts, she recognized the familiar landmarks—St Clement Danes, her tube station, the teashop where she had lunched, usually on sausage roll and cocoa—the whole panorama of those early days flashed back upon her with a quick and exquisite nostalgia. How little, despite the march of progress and the jam of panting vehicles which now encumbered the streets, how little it had changed!

Avoiding the obvious, she showed Madden over the precincts of the Inns of Court, the gatehouse on which Ben Jonson worked, the chapel where the curfew bell is still rung each night. Then they went through the Church of St Mary-le-Strand, where, in her lunch hour, she had often wandered. Madden, as he phrased it, fell for this church. But Katharine did not linger. Her mind and steps seemed bent involuntarily towards the end of Holborn, and at last, with a little constriction of her heart, she led the way into Staple Inn Courtyard. One second they were encompassed by the turmoil of the clashing street, and the next they were in this tranquil backwater, fronted by the venerable façade of the inn, soothed by the chirrup of sparrows in the elm above them. Beyond the outer traffic mutter the quiet was absolute, the sole movement the sleepy pecking of a few pigeons among the cobblestones.

"This is wonderful," said Madden slowly as they sat down on a bench. "In the very heart of London. I've read about it somewhere—yes, it comes into *Edwin Drood*, doesn't it? Yes, it's wonderful. And what a place to dream in!"

"I used to think so," Katharine answered.

He looked at her sharply, struck by the queerness of her voice. For a minute he was silent, then in a tone less casual than usual he said:

"I've noticed—couldn't help it, I suppose—that all this place round about means something to you. Why don't you tell me?"

"There's nothing to tell, really." She forced a smile. "When I was seventeen or eighteen, I worked pretty near. I used to come and sit here sometimes, in my off time, on this very bench. You see, it's just the usual sentimental nonsense. Why should I inflict it on you?"

"Because I want you to," he persisted. "I'm interested to hear how you began. I guess I'd understand. I had a pretty mean time myself when I first stepped out."

She could not understand her own weakness, an acquiescence induced by some strange evocation of the scene, yet almost before she knew it she was re-creating for herself, as much as for him, the sentimental images of her girlhood. Above, the sky held a quiet, warm glow. The afternoon was unusually mild. At their feet the pigeons pecked and strutted. The low beat of the City came from without like surf on a distant shore.

At first her words were rather halting, but the very sympathy of his audition seemed to give them shape and colour. She had begun as a typist with the firm of Twiss and Wardrop. At home circumstances were straitened, poverty lurking beneath the thin veneer of suburban respectability, and her father, who combined the attributes of an unsuccessful house agent with those of a vehement lay preacher, had found her this post. A hard, embittered man with a stony frown and an icy smile, he had small sympathy with her and no hope, however contemptuous, of her advancement. Twiss, a fellow Congregationalist, was taking her as 'a favour'.

It was this, perhaps, which had first set the seal on her endeavour and steeled her young sensitiveness against the world. She would show them at home—her father, everyone. A great ambition germinated. To and from her work she hurried, in black cotton stockings and skimpy skirt, under-nourished, but eager and alert. The great throbbing pulse of London was her unfailing stimulus. She watched with wide eyes the manifestations of wealth and luxury; returning late from the poky office, she would stand outside Covent Garden in the rain to see the arrival of famous personages. And meanwhile she plugged away at her typing, her shorthand, her book-keeping. She won golden opinions from Mr Twiss and even from the exacting Mr Wardrop. Her wages were raised once, twice, until she was earning the incalculable sum of two pounds, five shillings a week. Her father received the news with scornful incredulity.

And then, after four years, when she was only twenty-two, opportunity came. Old Eugene Hart, whose antique business lay quite near in Oxford Street, stopped her in the shop one day and asked her to become his private secretary at a salary of two hundred pounds a year. Old Eugene was a Jew, dark, benevolent and famously shrewd, who came frequently to the establishment of Twiss and Wardrop for those interesting transactions connected with the restoration, and sometimes—though this was barely whispered—the complete creation, of the antique. He had noted Katharine often from the corner of his inscrutable eye and divined, with the unerring instinct of his race, her potentialities.

It was a wrench for her to leave the shop in Holborn, yet the avenue opened by Hart's offer was enticing and immediate. Since her duties did not confine her entirely to her desk, she began to learn the 'trade', to know old furniture, its period and mark, to recognize at a glance the true patina of age. She attended sales everywhere with Hart, from Vernon's in the West End to great country houses in the North. And soon, since her aptitude was so evident and his health on the decline, he allowed her to go alone.

Buying for Hart was not only a responsibility—she would never forget her first trembling bid amid a multitude, it seemed, of hard-faced, hard-hatted dealers!—but it gave her also a definite cachet. She became, if not important, at least an interesting figure in the antique world. She saved money, too, for presently Hart added a commission to her salary, and this, especially when she made a fortunate purchase, reached quite a handsome total every month. But above everything, she fell in love with her profession, its glamour, possibilities and scope.

Three years later Eugene Hart died. Katharine, to whom he had been such a marvellous friend, was desolate. When the stock was sold by order of the executors and the business finally shut down, she felt like giving up her whole career. At this point, too, when she was most vulnerable, there came an added and unsettling persuasion from without. She had become acquainted with a young solicitor named Cooper, who was rising steadily in his own profession. George Cooper was an honest, plodding, likeable young man. In upbringing and tradition he was, like herself, respectable middle class, a stratum into which he had been born and in which, with a certain professional solidity, he would undoubtedly remain. They went about together, Katharine and he, in a quiet way, and she liked him greatly. He, on his part, was in love with her. And now he proposed marriage.

The temptation to Katharine was enormous. Twenty-five years

of age, the blood pounding healthily in her veins, momentarily, at least, halted in the march of her career, and unhappy at home, where her father, now turned an old, complaining invalid, often made life unbearable. How happy she could be in her own house, with her husband, her children! Tenderness rushed over her at the thought. How hard and solitary seemed the other road and how unlikely now to lead towards success!

The decision was a terrible one for her. And George, not without insistence, was pressing her to let him have her answer. The day came, a wintry day like this, when she must make her choice, that predestined choice between career and home. Perplexed and sad, she took her troubles to this old courtyard and sat on the bench under the tree, battling her problem out. When she arose, it was quite dark, but her mind was made up. Her career must come first. Always, always, it must be her career. That night she wrote refusing George Cooper and at the same time applied for the assistant editorship of the *Collector*, a monthly magazine devoted to furniture, decoration, and the fine arts.

One week later she was on the staff of the *Collector*, and one year later she was its editor-in-chief. Thereafter she had stepped off into space as Antika Ltd, her own mistress in her own business. Up and up she had gone. She had made distinguished friends, had become something of a figure in London and New York. Of course she had met with difficulties; who had not? Yet she had made large sums of money. And she had spent them. She had been able to do something for her mother, for Nancy. She had been—yes, if the word meant anything, she had been a success.

There was a long silence when she had finished. Then without looking at her, Madden deliberately took her hand, gave it a firm clasp, and relinquished it.

"I'm glad, and honoured, you've told me that, Katharine. But I guess there's just one guy I'm sorry for."

"Who?" she demanded.

"George Cooper," he answered slowly. "I guess he knew all right what he missed."

She smiled a trifle sadly. "He didn't miss much. Besides, he's married now, I expect, and perfectly happy on his own account."

Perhaps he discerned the sadness in her face, that gentle melancholy which memories always bring, for with a quick glance at his watch he rose briskly.

"It's well past teatime. And you're half-frozen from sitting here. You're coming now to that bun shop you used to go to, and you're going to drink three cups of scalding tea."

Now it was he who seemed to be in command of the excursion, for he steered her through the traffic to that A.B.C. she had once known so well. Inside it was warm and bright, the big plated urn on the counter hissed and steamed, the long wall mirrors reflected the bustling waitresses and the little groups eating, laughing, chattering at the round marble-topped tables. They had immense cups of tea and hot buttered toast.

"This," said Katharine, "is good." Still munching, she glanced at herself in a mirror and tucked a strand of hair under her hat, which had as usual fallen back from her forehead. "Heavens, what a fright I look!" Her lips twitched. "I deserve it. So does any woman who tells the story of her life."

"I asked for it, didn't I? Some day I'll tell you mine."

Her smile widened. "Don't tell me you sold newspapers in the streets of Cleveland."

He grinned. "Sure! Only it was peanuts instead of newspapers."

"And you went barefoot?"

"All the time!" He finished the last of his toast methodically. "But the only thing that worries me now is that I've got to hang around by myself all evening. You've no idea how lost I am without Nancy. I guess I'm counting the minutes till she comes down on Sunday." He paused. "You wouldn't—you wouldn't care to continue to take pity on me and come to a show?" Quickly he produced the evening paper which he had bought outside and ran his finger down the column. "There are some good pieces here by the looks of them."

"You can't tell by the looks of them," said Katharine.

She felt on the whole that her obligation towards him had, for the day at least, ceased. She did not much care to go to the theatre, yet she followed his finger down the list until it reached the Savoy Theatre, where, she observed with a pleasurable start, there was taking place a revival of Gilbert and Sullivan. The opera this evening was *Iolanthe*.

"*Iolanthe!*" she exclaimed almost involuntarily.

He raised his eyes. "You'd like that?"

She coloured slightly, and after a pause she explained. "Now *I'm* being naïve. But I love Gilbert and Sullivan. Perhaps all the more because when I wanted to go, I seldom could. I used to sit here in this very tea shop, longing with all my soul to cram into the pit or the gallery for *Pinafore* or *The Mikado* or *Iolanthe*. But there was night school, or night work to be done. I just couldn't go."

"Well, you'll go to-night," he declared emphatically and called out to the waitress for the bill.

They got seats easily, rather far back, which made less conspicuous the fact that they had not dressed. The orchestra tuned up, then broke into the overture. The curtain rose. Katharine surrendered herself to an immense delight.

It was a genuine treat for her. Often she was obliged to attend the first nights of smart revues and modern musical comedies, but she had little taste for their rapid nonstop rhythms. This was different. It chimed with her mood. It was witty and tuneful. Did it date? She did not know, nor did she care. At the risk of being out-moded she had the courage to like it openly.

Madden also liked it. She could see that. He did not say much. He had no comments to make between the scenes. He did not bother her with inane offers of coffee or ice cream during the intervals. He sat for the most part with his cheek in his palm and his elbow on the arm of the stall, his body still, his dark eyes, amused and interested, fixed steadily on the stage. But when it was all over and they came out of the auditorium and stood waiting for a taxi, he declared quickly:

"That's another treat I have to thank you for." He added: "Nancy'll be real pleased you've been so good to me. I'll tell her the minute she gets back."

Katharine smiled. "It's you who have entertained me."

"Oh, no," he replied quickly. "I'm a poor hand at entertaining. And I guess I've had less than usual to say to-night. As a matter of fact I've been wondering how things are working out up in Manchester."

They both thought of Nancy as they drove to Curzon Street. When the taxi came to rest, she asked him to come and have a drink before returning to his hotel. He accepted. They took the lift and entered the flat. A telegram lay upon the salver in her tiny hall. She ripped it open. It said:

SHOW A COMPLETE FLOP LONDON OPENING INDEFINITELY POSTPONED MEANING ALTOGETHER WASHED OUT EXPECT ME TOMORROW LOVE TEARS AND CURSES NANCY.

Concern flooded his face instantly. He bit his lip and took the telegram from her hand. "Poor kid. That's just too bad," he muttered when he had re-read it. "I didn't want her to quit the thing that way!"

Almost at once, as if forgetful of the fact that he was her guest, he took a hurried good-bye of Katharine.

Chapter Six

It was ten o'clock on Sunday morning when Nancy appeared at Curzon Steet. She had travelled down overnight, curled up in the corner of a third-class compartment, a small, solitary, disconsolate figure. The rest of the company had remained to make the journey comfortably by day, but she had felt that she must get away at once. The failure of the play upon which she had built so high had upset her frightfully. As the train pounded through the darkness, her face, set and wan, expressed the reality of her disappointment. Her usual air of flippancy, that gay little mask she usually presented to the world, was gone. Those who judged Nancy from that brilliant, hard exterior ought really to have seen her there. She looked a very wretched little child indeed.

And yet before she reached London she had pulled herself together. She might, in her own idiom, be completely sunk, but not for anything would she show it. She made good her face, which the journey's grime, and perhaps a stray tear, had slightly ravaged. And later, at the flat, she made an operatic little entry, advancing with her arms outstretched to where Katharine sat in a dark silk dressing gown over a belated morning tray of coffee and hot toast.

"Darling Katharine," she cried, as though years had separated them. "It's so lovely to see you again!" She touched her cheek against Katharine's, jerked a cushion out of the way, sat down on the couch beside her, and smiled brightly. "I've had such a fiend's own time up north."

Katharine, with a practical gesture, drew the tray towards them. "Have some breakfast, then, and tell me all about it."

"Darling!" Nancy gave a histrionic little shudder. "I couldn't eat a single morsel. I'm too incredibly upset."

"What! Haven't you had anything this morning?"

"Nothing, nothing! Only an omelette or something, toast and orange juice—oh, I forget." She dismissed her diet, between tragedy and petulance. "I had to fly round, simply fly round, to tell you."

"You've seen Chris, of course."

"Yes," Nancy nodded. "He's been sweet, wonderfully sweet—met me at the station, took me to John Street. But I wanted you, Katharine. I wanted to talk to you alone."

"All right," Katharine said comfortingly. In an unobtrusive fashion she poured out a fresh cup of coffee, sugared and creamed it, and placed it before the abandoned Nancy. "As a matter of fact, I expected you'd be round. But you're not to worry yourself about the play."

"Play!" declared Nancy with a grimace of antipathy. "I wish it had been a play! And yet I don't know. Perhaps it was, perhaps it would have been, a play if that Renton woman hadn't killed it. She massacred it, laid it out on a slab dead as mutton. She's hopless. She can't act. She never could act. And in any case she's far too old. Oh, if only I'd had that part, Katharine! Although I was pretty good, thank you, in my own, I'd have sailed through it. At least I'd have given the beastly show a chance. Oh, Katharine! I did so want a thumping West End run. It's just the exact point in my career when I could do with it." With a sudden access of vexation Nancy raised the cup of coffee and drank it.

Suppressing a smile, Katharine studied her niece. Despite the rigours of that nocturnal train ride she had never looked more attractive than she did this morning, in this moment of emotion which owed something to reality and something, she was not too fond to admit, to artifice. Yes, there was no doubt, Katharine decided, that now Nancy was enjoying a little of her own dramatic effects. And certainly they suited her.

"It is a pity, perhaps," Katharine said at length. "But does it matter as much as all that?"

"Of course it does." Nancy sat up with indignation. "What an idiotic question, Katharine!"

"I was just thinking," Katharine returned mildly, "of our friend Madden."

"Darling," protested Nancy. "I see what you mean and all that. I adore Chris. But I adore the theatre, too. And I owe something to myself as well, to the artist in me. You know how beautifully I've got on; I've been really *quick*. And now this flop at the most critical time! Oh, I know it was a stupid play. It deserved to fail. But I was in the failure, and I can't run away from it. That would be too cowardly." She jumped up and began to pace the room. "Oh, no, *no*, Katharine darling. That would be a complete anticlimax. I want to marry Chris, but I've got to be a success. I've got to justify myself, as well. Oh, I want to succeed, succeed, *succeed*!"

"I see," said Katharine.

There was a pause. Nancy, arrested in her pacing, turned with a new expression and a sudden and appealing change of manner. "There's only one thing we can do about it," she murmured, fixing Katharine with a gaze now clear and ingenuous, and holding her pose—Duse, Terry, and Bernhardt bound into one. "You've got to help me."

"But how, Nancy?"

"Don't look at me as if I were unhinged, darling. You know how."

"You mean you want to get into another play?"

"Exactly!" Nancy relaxed, sighed, and, finding herself near the piano, sat down and struck a slow, persuasive chord. "In this particular instance, Katharine," she remarked gently, "you can step in very neatly. You've got such influence—to be completely vulgar, such wonderful pull, darling—with everybody—with Sam Bertram in particular."

"Why Bertram?"

"Because"—Nancy struck another chord—"because Bertram is taking *Dilemma* to New York—his new show, Katharine, in case you don't know. Because Bertram hasn't cast it yet. Because Bertram is going to give a really nice part in it to me."

"Oh, no, Nancy, that's impossible," Katharine said quickly. "I couldn't ask him."

"You must, darling," said Nancy, using the loud pedal by way of emphasis. "Unless you want me to be shattered and miserable for life."

"But really . . ." protested Katharine.

"You must," repeated Nancy. "There's a part in *Dilemma* that's just crying out for me. Not large, darling, but right, just absolutely right. I could raise the dead with that part. But that's the least of it. I want to go to America with you. I want to go with Chris. He's got to get back, darling, back to his business. He wants me to go with him and marry him there. Don't you see what a wonderful thing it would be if you could get me into Bertram's show? Simplifies everything. We all go together and have the most divine time."

Katharine gazed at Nancy, still taken aback, and conscious through it all that she had been skilfully played upon by this amazing contradiction of guile and ingenuousness, by this mixed-up, clever little niece of hers. In spite of herself a spark of amusement danced into her eyes.

"You seem to have planned it all very thoroughly."

"But of course, darling."

"It doesn't quite follow that Bertram's going to be as easy as I am."

"But you'll ask him," cried Nancy quickly.

There was a pause while Katharine's expression relented further. "All right," she said at last.

"You darling!" With a final crashing chord Nancy rose from the piano and flung her arms round Katharine's neck. "Oh, I knew you'd do it. I counted on you. I'm so happy! I know that when you take a thing in hand, it's as good as done."

She drew back, contemplating Katharine with sincere affection and gratitude. She hugged her again, then switched her regard towards the tiny platinum watch on her wrist. Immediately her look became regretful.

"And now I must fly. I promised to meet Chris at eleven. He's such a dear I hate to keep him waiting. Go to-day, won't you, Katharine—to Bertram? Or to-morrow if he's not in town. Good-bye, darling, and thanks a million."

When Nancy had gone, Katharine stood for a minute in rather mixed reflection. One part of her observed that Nancy was making kind yet calculating use of her, the other acknowledged that no demand of Nancy's could ever overtax the willing service of her love. It was true she had some influence with Bertram and, if Nancy's information were correct, might possibly persuade him. Though it cost her independent nature dear to ask such a favour, she felt that Nancy was relying on her, that she must do it for her sake. At this her brow cleared, and with an impulsive movement she went to the telephone. She hardly expected Bertram to be in London at the week-end, but from Winter, his man, she could at least find out his engagements for the coming week.

It was, in fact, Winter's voice that answered—his booming tones were unmistakable—yet when Katharine made her inquiry, he answered, with some slight hesitancy and a suggestion of mystery, that his master was at home.

"Good!" exclaimed Katharine. "Then tell him, Winter, that I'm coming round to see him."

"Oh, no, Miss Lorimer," protested Winter. "You can't possibly see him."

"But why? He isn't engaged all day."

"I'm afraid so, Miss Lorimer. You see, he's—he's indisposed."

"Indisposed?" Winter's manner was baffing Katharine. She demanded outright: "What's wrong with him?"

Silence of hesitation at the other end. Then, with majestic reluctance: "If you must know, Miss Lorimer, Mr Bertram has toothache."

There was something so sepulchral in Winter's pronouncement of the malady that Katharine had to laugh. Quickly, rather than hurt his feelings, which she knew to be highly organized, she hung up the receiver. But her intention to make the visit remained, since if something were to be done for Nancy, it had better be done at once.

Towards three o'clock, therefore, by which time she judged Bertram's neuralgia might have subsided, she left her flat and set off briskly in the direction of Portman Square.

She pressed the doorbell at No. 16a, and Winter answered her ring in person, standing tall, thin, and funereal above her.

"I'm sorry, Miss Lorimer," he began, and she saw that he was uncertain about admitting her.

But before he could summon his decision she was in the hall, smiling at him reassuringly, murmuring:

"It's all right, Winter, I'll find my way in!"

She marched past the perturbed manservant towards the study, which, from her familiarity with Bertram's habits, she knew must now contain him.

In this she was right, but more by chance than judgment, for Bertram was not working at his desk but sat instead, in a plaid dressing gown, crouched over a heaped coal fire, his head encased in a Shetland shawl, his attitude the ludicrous personification of misery.

"Why, Bertie!" exclaimed Katharine spontaneously. "Is it as bad as all that?"

"Worse," he mumbled. Then after a silence he painfully screwed round his head and surveyed her with a jaundiced eye. "What the devil are you doing here?"

Though her heart went out to him in sympathy, there was about him in his present situation, dishevelled, beshawled, and swollen-cheeked, something so irresistibly reminiscent of the comic strip that Katharine had to fight down an awful tremor of mirth. Hurriedly she declared:

"I just dropped in for a minute. And I'm so glad I came. You must let me do something for you."

"You can't," he mumbled mournfully. "I don't want to be disturbed. I told Winter."

"It wasn't Winter's fault. And look here, Bertie. . ."

"Can't look anywhere," he interrupted. "Toothache, damnable

face-ache. Let me alone. I couldn't buy an antique now to save my life."

"I haven't come here to sell you an antique."

"You haven't come here for nothing. I know you. On a Sunday, too. Out you get, Katharine!"

"No, I won't," she answered determinedly, and took a step towards him. "It's absurd to see you suffering like this. Haven't you seen a dentist?"

"Hate dentists. Never had any time for them. Hate the whole crew. Besides ..." he groaned delicately, held rigid by a sudden wave of his affliction. When it had subsided, he lay back, spent, on the chair and explained: "Abscess, I think. Can't inject. Can't do anything."

"You can have it out," said Katharine in some astonishment.

"Out!" He jumped, almost, in his chair. "Without an injection? In cold blood? Out! Oh, Lord, does the woman think I'm made of iron? Out! Oh, dear Lord, forgive her!"

With a shudder he turned his back and, holding the afflicted cheek tenderly, began to rock himself gently to and fro.

Katharine studied him with genuinely affectionate concern, reflecting, perhaps a little tritely yet none the less truly in the circumstances, how like children men could be, especially when bereft of feminine government. She exclaimed:

"Let me have a look at it, Bertie."

"No, thanks."

"But you must. It's too ridiculous for you to go on suffering."

Firmly she advanced towards him. His eyes, sole mobility of his stricken face, rotated towards her wildly. But she was too much for him. Crouched like a spaniel threatened by the whip, he groaned again and surrendered, opening his mouth, exposing a dark stump of molar set in an area of angry gum.

When she had satisfied herself as to the trouble, Katharine took up her place on the hearthrug and contemplated him severely. "Look here, Bertie, it's insanity leaving this. You've got to have it out at once."

"You can't," he remonstrated feebly. "You can't inject. . . ."

"Gas," returned Katharine laconically.

He paled under the shawl, which with an effort of self-preservation he had resumed. "Gas?"

"Yes, gas, Bertie!"

He made a last effort to escape. "I can't have an anaesthetic. The very idea's enough for me. I've never had an anaesthetic in my life."

"Well, you will now," said Katharine in her most final and formidable tone. "I'm going to phone up Dr Blake, and you're going to have this wretched tooth out right away."

"No, no. Don't you dare! If I have gas, I'll pass out for good. I'm better . . . I'm absolutely all right now. Oh! Oh. . .!"

He was struggling up in his chair, protesting, when another wave of anguish caught him and laid him back again, vanquished and at her mercy.

Katharine eyed her old friend with a compassionate yet unrelenting gaze; then she went out of the room and down to the hall, where she rang Dr Blake, her own surgeon dentist, who lived just round the comer in Queen Anne Street, and asked him to come round at once. From Winter, who hovered near, a troubled and cadaverous shadow, she demanded hot water and clean towels.

Katharine remained in the hall until Dr Blake arrived.

"You must be firm, Doctor," she admonished him. "No nonsense about putting this off."

"Not on your life, Miss Lorimer," he answered with a smile. "I never put off till to-morrow what ought to come out to-day."

Upstairs they found the wretched victim prostrate with the premonition of his fate, too far gone even to raise a feeble protest. It took barely a minute to prepare the apparatus. Bertram darted one look at its dark cylinders and coils of red tubing and shivered as if chilled by an icy blast.

"You're going to finish me," he muttered. "I'll never come through it."

"Rot!" said Blake breezily.

"Don't I—don't I want a special chair or something?" faltered Bertram.

"Not on your life," said Blake more breezily than ever. It seemed to be a favourite expression. He rolled up his right cuff expertly. "Just loosen your collar and sit up pretty."

A ghastly grin spread over Bertram's face. "Sit up pretty," he cackled. "If I wasn't a dying man, I would laugh."

Here the door opened, and Winter entered, stepping gravely forward with a basin in his hand like a surgeon apothecary bent on blood. It was the last straw. Bertram shut his eyes tight. As Blake slipped the rubber mask over his face, he blubbered:

"Hold my hand, Katharine. And for God's sake hold it tight."

Three minutes later he opened his eyes and stared glassily at Blake, who, whistling gently, was re-packing his instruments. Winter and the basin had vanished, and so, it dawned on Bertram, had the tooth, the agony, the nightmare in its entirety. The miracle overcame him. He remained passive until the dentist had gone. Then he sat up and considered Katharine with a slow, unpainful smile.

"It's you," he declared. He reassured himself as to his relief by tapping his cheek; then he smiled again, rather sheepishly. "Wonderful stuff, that gas. I was pretty plucky about it, though, wasn't I?"

"You were splendid, Bertie."

"I wasn't . . . Oh, well, hang it all, it isn't a very pleasant thing to face up to. It isn't everybody who would do it. I mean the anaesthetic and everything."

"Yes, you did marvellously. It was a quite nasty tooth."

Here, following her gaze, he discovered the tooth, which lay on a swab of cotton wool on the table beside him. He picked it up and contemplated it with pride.

"Well! Well! A great septic molar, too. Better out than in, eh, Katharine? Thank the Lord I had the nerve to go through with it."

Looking up suddenly, he caught her steady gaze upon him, and all at once he paused like a boy detected in the jam cupboard. He gave a guilty blink. His face fell slowly. Then his eyes twinkled, and with real enjoyment he began to laugh. He laughed a long time.

"Oh, Lord, Katharine, what a funk I was in! And what a brick you were to force me into it. If you hadn't, I'd still be suffering blue hell!" He reached out and pressed the bell. "Now we're going to have some tea. I'm hungry. My appetite's ferocious. Would you believe it, I haven't had a thing all day!"

She shook her head. "No, I'm going to have the tea, Bertie. You're going to have some nice, nourishing soup."

"Ha! Ha! Good idea. I need nourishment. I feel as if I'd eaten nothing for a week."

Later, when Winter had padded in and out, and Bertram, with a napkin tucked round his chin, was splashing his way through a bowl of bouillon, he suddenly declared:

"You know, Katharine, you've missed your vocation. You ought to have been a nurse or a doctor. No, on my oath, you ought to have been somebody's wife. Mine, for example." He waved his spoon vigorously. "That's an idea. Marry me, Katharine, and make an honest man of me at last."

She simply smiled at him, taking no notice, and he ran on:

"What *can* I do for you, then, if I'm no use to you as a husband? Only one thing's impossible. You mustn't try to sell me anything. I'm down to the bone over my new show."

Katharine took a deep breath. Though she would have deliberately broached the subject, this opening, together with his gratitude, gave her an opportunity she could not fail to take. "I do want to ask something of you, Bertie and it's over your new show. Give my niece, Nancy Sherwood, a part in it."

The intensity rather than the nature of her request drew him up. He finished his soup slowly. "Mmm," he said at length. "So that's it. She's put you up to it, Katharine. Clever little devil."

"She is clever, Bertie," Katharine said quickly. "And you know she can act."

"Yes," he admitted. "She's pretty good." He paused. "And she's

63

got pluck. I heard all about her little do at the B.B.C. the other day. Those things get around." He paused again. "Mmm! But suppose we wait a bit. In a year or two she'll have more experience."

"There won't be a year or two," Katharine declared earnestly. "She'll be married and settled down long before that. She wants to make good now—you know how it is, Bertie—to feel that she's not a failure, to finish with the knowledge of having done something."

He looked at her askance. "Oh, yes?"

"Besides," she went on quickly, "I want her to be in America when I'm there. It's got to do with her future, her happiness, with everything that really matters."

There was a silence. He stroked his chin reflectively and was some time before replying, but at last he took a sudden decision. "All right, Katharine; for your sake I'll do it. There's a good part she can have. It'll suit Nancy down to the ground. It's hers. Tell here to look me up at the office to-morrow."

Her face flooded with a warm colour. Delighted, she rose and took both his hands. "Thank you, Bertie!" she cried. "That's something I'll never forget."

"That's all right. Come to think of it, Nancy'll make a good set-off to Paula Brent, who's playing lead."

His manner, deliberately offhand, did not conceal his gratification that she should be pleased.

Shortly afterward she took her leave. An indescribable elation filled her as she walked home, bent on telephoning Nancy the instant she reached Curzon Street. Her American visit took on a new complexion, was coloured by a vivid sense of anticipation. She had always wanted to take the trip with Nancy. And it was, she reflected with a little inward glow, in some strange fashion an added happiness that Madden would be going, too.

Chapter Seven

The Forenoon of their departure was raw and foggy, with infrequent blinks of a dull red sun which loomed like a heavy eye upon the rim of the yellow sky.

There were four of them in the reserved compartment as the train tore its passage to Southampton through stretches of dreary chimney pots, for Charley Upton had the sentimental habit of seeing Katharine off on her transoceanic ventures.

Madden and Upton, in opposite corners, were getting acquainted through the medium of a polite conversation on the merits of the American football game, while Nancy, her fur coat upon the rack and her new dressing case beside her, ran excitedly through the illustrated weeklies in the hope of finding pictorial news of her intimates or herself. It had been a disappointment to her that Bertram and the rest of the *Dilemma* company were not coming on the Pindaric, but sailing two days later on the *Imperial*, a faster and, as Nancy did not fail to indicate, a smarter ship. But now she had got over it—in her own phrase, recovered from the blow.

Katharine was unusually lighthearted, pervaded by a glow of optimism, and acute appreciation of the fact, evident yet sometimes overlooked, that it was good to be alive. Also, it was good to have friends—Bertram in particular had been extraordinarily kind—and to be going away with Madden and Nancy. Her thoughts raced ahead. In these next few weeks she would sell the miniature to Brandt, bring her business worries to an end, see Nancy's happiness assured. Suddenly she became aware of her niece leaning towards her.

"Look Katharine," said Nancy with a conscious little laugh. "They've shoved in this of me. Do you think it's good?"

Turning, Katharine studied the illustration which Nancy held out to her, a recent and very lovely studio portrait. It was a profile taken from an odd angle and lighted most strikingly, the chin uptilted, the hair flung back, winged like the head of a flying Hermes.

"Yes, it's terribly good," Katharine acquiesced warmly. "And quite original."

"It's not vanity," said Nancy suddenly. "It's just that it's important from my point of view. You know, keeping oneself before the public and all that."

Madden and Upton both admired the photograph, Upton especially commenting on the likeness.

"This question of likeness," Katharine interposed on an impulse, "it's very queer how it turns out." After a moment she continued: "For example, here's something that people have said is like me. How it can be I don't know. But you can judge for yourselves."

Snapping open the small jewel case which lay beside her, she produced the miniature and offered it for their inspection. In a sudden silence the tiny Holbein went from hand to hand.

Madden looked at it a long time, then with an intake of his breath he declared: "It certainly is like you, Katharine. And it's a darn lovely little picture, too."

Upton, peering over Madden's shoulder, agreed, and added: "How much is that going to cost some infatuated American?"

"Twenty thousand pounds," Katharine smiled, "I hope."

"And I wouldn't say it wasn't worth it," said Madden seriously. "It's got real class."

At her end of the compartment Nancy laughed. "Perhaps you're thinking of having it yourself, Chris," she suggested.

"Sure," Madden answered pleasantly.

Then he smiled and handed back the miniature to Katharine, who locked it back in her case.

At this point Upton looked at his watch, an action less habitually dependent on the passage of time than on Charley's cordial inclination towards food or drink. "What about a spot of luncheon?" he inquired. "I'm pretty sharp set myself. I've ordered it for twelve o'clock. We've got a special table in the dining car."

The lunch, which was extremely good, passed off cheerfully. Katharine's spirits were still soaring, and she kept the conversation bowling merrily.

Soon, however, Southampton drew upon them, and almost immediately they ran into the harbour station, where a long line of stewards in white jackets and peaked caps stood at attention with the high black wall of the *Pindaric* rising sheer behind. Though no longer strange, something in the spectacle, the portent of adventure, the prelude to another crossing of that great mysterious ocean, evoked an answer of excitement in Katharine. Familiarity had not staled the sensation for her. Out on the platform she sniffed the sea air with a lively anticipation, and, taking Nancy affectionately by the arm, led the way up the covered gangway to the ship.

It was in a sense a triumphal progress. Katharine had travelled by the *Pindaric* so often that the whole ship's company knew her and greeted her with that immediate and deferential recognition which was sweet as honey to the knowledgeable little Nancy, since she shared it.

"Do you own this ship, by any chance?" she inquired as they marched along the alleyway behind one of the pursers and a procession of stewards.

"If I do, it's yours," Katharine answered, smiling.

They had large cabins, with a communicating door, on C deck. Madden's was on the starboard side, opposite, farther aft. At once Nancy was engaged by the collection of telegrams, messages, and flowers which awaited them, while Katharine talked to Mrs Robbins, the stewardess who invariably looked after her. A moment later Mr Pym, the chief purser, came along. He was a portly red-faced man with protuberant eyes and in addition a slight squint which he cleverly turned into a sidelong beaming look.

"Well, well," he declared, holding Katharine's hand in his with an air of happy privilege, "it's fine to have you with us again, Miss Lorimer. And you've brought your niece, too. I hope we'll have a good crossing. Anything I can do, Miss Lorimer, you know you've only got to say the word."

"You can put this in your safe for a start," said Katharine, taking the miniature from her case.

He accepted it with fitting respect. "Ah, yes, I read about your purchase, Miss Lorimer. You may trust me to take care of it." He rubbed his hands together softly and retreated sideways, like a benign crab, towards the door. "Meanwhile I'll send you along a little fruit. Nothing nicer in the cabin than a little fruit."

This was a famous aphorism of the famous Mr Pym, but repeated only to his favoured guests. He had, in fact, scarcely gone before a steward arrived bearing a basket of the most lovely hothouse fruits.

"How do you do it, darling?" Nancy reflected airily. "Service for ladies. Reception a la duchesse. Everything too marvellous."

Katharine's expression altered at Nancy's tone. "I don't know," she answered rather shortly. "I don't ask them to do it. And they know there's precious little of the duchess about me."

"Nothing nicer," continued Nancy in a perfect burlesque of the chief purser, "than a little fruit in the cabin. And your niece, too. She's fond of fruit, I trust? Ah! I hope you'll have a nice crossing. With a little fruit in the cabin." She laughed, that sharp little laugh in which there seemed a hidden scratch. "Isn't he a ridiculous old bird, Katharine?"

But Katharine did not laugh. She reddened, and for a second her brows drew down. "I don't like that, Nancy," she said steadily. "The old bird, as you call him, is one of my best friends. He's shown me endless kindness since I made my first trip. I was not much older than you then, but too shy and nervous to speak to a soul. He took me in hand and introduced me to people. He helped me find my feet. He was decent to me. And he always has been decent. As for his being ridiculous, a great many famous people, I may tell you, are glad to call Pym their friend. He's a real person."

"Darling Katharine," cried Nancy instantly, her cheapness gone, her whole attitude apologetic. "I didn't mean anything. I didn't know you felt that way about him. As for his kindness, and all this attention, it's gorgeous—simply wonderful for me."

There was a pause, then Katharine's smile broke through again.

"That's all that matters, then. I knew you couldn't mean it. And if you're happy, so am I."

A few minutes later they went up to the promenade deck, where Upton stood with Madden awaiting them. Now the imminence of departure was in the air. Already a steward was beating the gong. People began to move towards the gangways.

"I'll have to be going presently," said Upton with quite a prodigious sigh. "Promise me you'll take care of yourself and all that, Katharine."

"Of course I will, Charley."

He looked so woebegone, as he always did on such occasions, that her heart went out to him. His devotion to her was so constant, undemanding, and so absurdly sentimental it sometimes moved her, as it did now, to an impulse of real tenderness.

"Dash it all," he went on, "I always feel so dismal when you're away. If you're gone too long this time, hanged if I don't take another trip over and fetch you back."

A long blast on the ship's siren and a throb of life vibrating through the hull expedited an awkward moment. Upton said good-bye to Nancy and Madden, then, pressing Katharine's hand in his, turned quickly and hurried down the gangway. Something rueful in his retreating figure plucked at Katharine. She moved away from Nancy and Madden, who now stood close together by the rail watching the slow edging of the ship from the quay, and climbed slowly to the boat deck above.

Here, on its deserted stretch, quite damp from the soft sea mist, she began to pace up and down, her mood fallen unexpectedly towards the verge of sadness. The ship, closely pinioned by two tugs, was veering gradually towards the Solent. Soon, however, a quicker and more powerful pulse activated her. The dun-coloured water rushed past with greater speed, the swooping gulls slipped far astern into the churning wake, the land began to fade. It was a moment curiously touching and impressive, and though Katharine did not break the spell by attempting to analyse her sensations, she had the impression of sweeping into another world whose shapes were phantomlike and sad. But its desolation, at last, was broken by a step matching her own. Swinging round, she found Madden beside her, and immediately her despondency dropped from her, and she was pervaded by a sense of comfort in his companionship.

"Nancy sent me up," he explained. "She's gone down below to straighten out."

She nodded, pacing beside him in friendly silence.

"Oughtn't you to have a coat on?" he asked at length. "It's cold for you up here."

"No, I like it," she answered.

Again there came a silence, which, as though bringing himself to it, he broke with disturbing suddenness.

"That fellow Upton," he began, "he's a good sort. He looks easy and slack, but he's a regular fellow for all that." He paused significantly. "And he's up to his ears in love with you."

Katharine, taken aback, made no reply, but continued to walk beside him.

"I've been figuring things out in my head," he went on, his expression meditative, even troubled. "It's pretty fair cheek on my part. I've known you only a short while, but that doesn't prevent me from feeling as if I'd known you all my life. And I can't help thinking. . ."

He broke off. Another pause. Stealing a glance at his worried face, which appeared, nevertheless, concentrated and full of purpose, she smiled faintly and inquired.

"Well?"

"Well, it's like this, Katharine. I've seen a good bit of you lately, and it's struck me you don't get as much out of life as you ought to. You're never tired of doing things for other people. It's give, give, give with you all the time, but—darn it all!—you never seem to *get*. Maybe it's because I'm so happy with Nancy I want you to be happy, too; I don't know. But I think it's time something was fixed up about you. I'm making too long a speech altogether! All I want to say is, why don't you marry Upton and let him take care of you for good?"

For a moment she did not answer. If anyone else had spoken to her on such a subject, she would have been deeply offended. But now she was not offended. She was half-nonplussed, half-pleased. It was, of course, ridiculous for him to talk to her like a grand-uncle, yet she could not help being moved by his obvious solicitude—or perhaps affection was the better word—for her.

"No," she replied at last, "I can't see myself letting poor Charley take care of me."

"Why not? He's rich enough."

"Does that matter?"

"I guess it helps some."

She shook her head. "It wouldn't help me. You see, I'm quite old-fashioned, incurably romantic, and dreadfully stupid. If I had made up my mind to marry, money wouldn't matter a scrap to me. It just happens that I don't love Charley."

Again there came a pause. Her answer drew him up, yet seemed to give him little satisfaction.

"Well," he said slowly, that vague frown still between his eyes, "if that's the case, you can't get past it."

"No," she answered quietly.

They walked the deck in silence after that, hearing the thrum of the wind against the superstructure of the deck and the sounding of the waves upon the hull far beneath them. Then, as the early darkness came upon them and the ship's lights broke out like stars, she left him and went below.

Chapter Eight

Dinner that evening was informal and unprolonged, since Captain Ireland never appeared on the first night out and none of the seasoned passengers troubled to change. But, judging by their table companions—Jay French, the cosmopolitan journalist, Edward Brett, an architect of international reputation, and Lady Blandwell, who was bent on her first lecture tour of the United States—the crossing promised to be amusing.

The next day came, and shipboard life began its measured yet exciting course. The sea, obedient to Mr Pym's injunction, was calm. Katharine fell into her usual routine as though she had known no other than a maritime existence. In the morning there was gymnasium, followed by a plunge in the swimming pool of Ionian marble—known euphoniously as the Olympian Bath. Nancy, inclined to indolence, would have lain abed, but Katharine, always a demon for exercise when afloat, dragged her up for medicine ball, a workout on the rowing machine, a gallop on the electric horse. After luncheon they wrapped themselves in rugs and lay in a sheltered nook of the promenade deck reading or watching the slow recession of the billows. Often, at Katharine's suggestion, they took tea there rather than in the orchestrated magnificence of the Palm Lounge. A cocktail before dinner and a motion-picture show afterward completed the easy order of the day.

Katharine's main object was to make the trip memorable for Nancy. Her own first crossing, as she had already indicated, had been an occasion of wonder and delight which lived imperishably in her recollection. Yet though she tried to bring to Nancy something of the same sensation, as time went on she could not repress a vague feeling of disappointment. Nancy seemed difficult to delight, and wonder was a quality she did not know. She was too young to be blasé. It was absurd that she should be bored. But her attitude to life appeared cool and unamazed. And for the first time it dawned on Katharine that although scarcely more than a decade separated the ages of Nancy and herself, they were divided, in point of character and outlook, by a gulf that might have been a generation.

Hurt, Katharine tried to bridge it. She fancied she might be offering more of her society to Madden and Nancy than they desired. Yet, though anxious now to leave them to themselves, she was always pressed into making a threesome of the party, which increased, more often than not, to quite a crowd. It was another of Nancy's attributes to insist on having people around her.

But Katharine was perhaps mistaken in her assumptions. Superficially Nancy had all the modern attributes, it is true, yet deep down there lay another, and a subtler, cause of her preoccupation. Her failure—for so she judged it—at Manchester had left a rankling wound, and now, subconsciously, her mind was fixed ahead, eager to wipe out the stigma of defeat by a great, a marvellous, success. Though saying nothing, she thought continually of her opening in New York, weighed minutely the possibilities of her part. She had the habit, too, of abruptly disappearing from view, usually in the evenings, for the purpose of studying her script. Her attitude was so casual no one thought much about these private vigils. Yet to Nancy they were vital and intense.

It so happened, then, on the evening of Thursday, the fourth day out, Nancy vanished to her cabin about nine o'clock, once more intent on her part, leaving Madden to take Katharine to the picture show alone. It was a dark and gusty night. The films, a knock-about comedy followed by a much scarred travelogue, were dull. Moreover, the swell, taking the ship abeam, had set up a slow, uncomfortable oscillation. These two circumstances combined to make the attendance sparse. Yet Katharine had never enjoyed herself so much. She sat in the semi-darkness, acknowledging the bright flicker upon the screen with the surface of her mind, happily aware of Madden's presence beside her and of the laboured yet exciting straining of the ship through the rising forces of the sea. Presently Madden turned to her with that smile she knew so well.

"Seems to be getting slightly rough," he murmured. "How do you feel?"

She shook her head, answering his smile with a glance of humorous hardihood. "Never felt better in my life."

"You don't want to go below?"

"Not unless you do!"

She was turning back gaily towards the screen when a sudden thought struck her and made her pause. Why should it please her to sit through this second-rate cinema performance in all the discomfort of a gale? She realized with a flash of dismay that it was because Madden was here. Yes, the last thing she desired was to surrender the curious elation of this moment. Her smile faded. She tried instinctively to think. But she had no time for that. Almost immediately complete and startling enlightenment came upon her.

He had put out his hand to steady her chair, which, un-battened, was now threatening to join the others in their foolish seesaw dance. And the next instant the ship yielded to an extra heavy roll which sent Katharine violently against him. Unbalanced, she lay in his arms, her cheek against his cheek, her breast against his side. For a few seconds he held her closely to prevent her falling while the ship hung over at an angle. Everything whirled about her, the ship, the sea, the universe itself. Then as the vessel righted itself he restored her gently to her seat.

"What do I get for that?" he inquired blandly. "The Albert medal for saving life at sea?"

She did not speak. To save her life she could not have uttered one word. She sat, pale to the lips, her body rigid, paralysed by that blinding revelation which had struck her, unsuspecting and defenceless, like a lightning stroke. She loved Madden. She loved him with her whole soul. Everything was clear, illumined and terrible, her joy in his society, her desire for his happiness, even her way of looking and hoping for his smile, all clear, clear and agonizing as a scene long hidden in darkness and now revealed by one electric

74

flash so white and burning it seared the unsuspecting eye. A deathly vertigo assailed her. She thought suddenly that she would faint. Clenching her hands fiercely, she fought the weakness off. She remained motionless, trembling within, unseeing, stricken.

At last the film wound itself out. The lights went on, and the survivors blinked at one another in mutual congratulation. Katharine, her head lowered, at once made her way towards the deck. Madden followed her. Outside she paused. Hardly anyone was about. The very quietness of the place made it more difficult for her. She could not look at him; she felt her soul must be naked in her eyes. And yet imposed upon her was the dreadful necessity of concealing everything, everything which ravaged her.

"I think I'll go below." How she forced her voice to a semblance of normality she never knew.

"Why go yet?" he answered, smiling. "You know Nancy begged us to leave her to study her part. Let's walk round the promenade deck."

His tone was perfectly natural. She could not judge whether he read her horrible distress. She kept her eyes averted, repeating:

"I must go down. It's getting late."

"It isn't that late, and we've hardly had any exercise to-day. And you like it, don't you, out on the deck, with the wind blowing guns?"

By the most incredible effort of her will she steeled herself to look at him. The friendly perplexity in his eyes hurt her dreadfully.

"You go yourself," she said. "Those stupid movies have tired me out."

"Well, if you feel that way about it," he smiled doubtfully, "I'll say good-night."

"Good-night." She made it natural at last; then, forcing her stiff lips to a casual smile, she turned and hurried towards the staircase, leaving him on the deck alone.

On C deck she paused, her hand against her throat, the thudding of her heart choking her. She could not face Nancy yet; she must first collect herself, firm her resolution into an irrevocable mould. The thought of Nancy gave her a new pain, wrung from the situation another pang. Quickly she went forward along the alleyway and out through the break of the forecastle. In the darkness she stumbled against winches and deck gear. She did not care. No physical hurt was comparable to the anguish of her mind. At last she reached the ship's bows, and there, clinging to the rail, her body swept and battered by the wind, her being encompassed by vast empty blackness and the formidable thunder of the sea, her soul cleft by an ecstasy of pain, she yielded finally to an agony of tears.

Chapter Nine

By the following morning the wind had blown itself out, the sky was bright, and the sea, though brisk, had moderated. At ten o'clock, when Nancy joined Madden on the promenade deck, she was unaccompanied by Katharine.

"Hello!" he exclaimed. "Where's the other partner?"

"Sleeping partner this morning," she rejoined brightly. "Headache!"

He considered her in some astonishment. "I heard her say the other day she never had a headache on board ship."

"Perhaps she didn't touch wood," said Nancy with a little laugh. "Don't gape, darling. Your beloved is perfectly fit and well."

He smiled down at her. "Then why didn't you turn up for gym?"

She made a grimace. She was in a smart, provoking mood, very different from her serious application of the previous evening. Reaction explained it, and a sense of well-being induced by the freshness of the morning. She answered happily:

"Don't bully me, darling. Not until we're married. Now be quiet and give me a cigarette."

"You won't smoke mine?" He raised an eyebrow at her. "I thought not! I shall have to get you some."

They took the lift to the main hall, where he ordered her a large box of her favourite cigarettes. As he gazed at her he thought that he had never seen her look more lovely. Slim, boyish, and audacious, her camel's-hair coat girded closely to her figure, she had a quality which made him catch his breath. Her soft curls were brushed to the back of her head. She was very busy putting on a great deal of lip rouge.

"You do love me, Nancy?" he said in a low voice.

She paused in what she was doing. Unexpectedly a deep wave of feeling came over her. All her flippancy fell from her. She caught her breath, realizing suddenly how much she cared for Chris, how much he meant to her. Gazing up at him seriously from under her lashes, she answered simply:

"With all my heart."

There was a pause. His face lit up. Quickly he grasped her hand. For a second their fingers touched, then with a little embarrassed laugh she broke away, striving to recapture her poise.

"Remember we're in mid-Atlantic," she declared lightly, and slipped her arm through his.

They stood for a minute studying the noticeboard, then, as they turned towards the staircase, his eye was taken by the florist's shop. A sudden notion struck him.

"By the bye! We ought to send some flowers to Katharine. It'll cheer her up."

"Grand idea," she agreed. "Send carnations. Katharine adores them. And look, darling, these lovely mauve orchids—aren't they super? I'm rather gone on them myself."

He gave her a quick glance, than laughed. Going into the shop, he ordered carnations to be sent to Katharine. The orchids Nancy carried off herself.

There was no sign of Katharine at lunch, and it was two o'clock before they came upon her in a sheltered section of the upper deck. She seemed snug in her long chair and wraps and perfectly tranquil, while the tray beside her indicated that she had eaten at least a sketchy meal.

"Hello, darling," Nancy sang out. "How's the head?"

"Much better." Katharine smiled up at them composedly from her rugs. She turned to Nancy. "I thought you were playing deck tennis."

"Yes, we're going along now. It's a bore, the competition. But you know Chris's feverish energy."

With a certain hesitancy Madden interposed. "We felt kind of worried about you, Katharine. Are you sure you're all right?"

"Perfectly. But I've been doing too much lately. I shall take it easy the rest of the trip."

He persisted, as though not yet satisfied: "It seemed so queer not seeing you at table to-day. And in the gym this morning—well, I missed you a lot."

"I'm sorry about that."

He stared at her, as though the quiet neutrality of her manner left him uncomfortably at a loss. Nancy, humming softly, had strolled away in the direction of the tennis courts, but he remained as though unwilling to leave the spot.

"You got the carnations we sent?"

"Why, yes, Chris." She paused. "But will you please not trouble to send me flowers again? Really, you mustn't."

He seemed even more perplexed. He still hesitated. Then he asked, as at a sudden idea: "Have I by any chance done anything to annoy you?"

Her glance travelled over his face, then away again. "Aren't we becoming a little involved about nothing at all this afternoon?" she murmured pleasantly. "Of course you've done nothing to annoy me. I'm just feeling as if I'd like to be alone for a bit."

He flushed. For a second the hurt expression lingered in his eyes. Then his face turned normal once again. "I'm sorry, Katharine," he said in a quiet voice. "I forgot about your headache. And I apologize for boring you."

He turned and walked after Nancy.

Katharine lay back in her chair, her book idle upon her lap, apparently absorbed by the remote consideration of sea and sky. No one could have guessed the pain that she endured, the weight which lay upon her heart, crushing and insufferable. It was as though, wilfully and of set design, she had plunged a knife into her own breast. She felt cold. All that remained to her was a tiny candle flame of comfort, the still white thought that she had begun what she had resolved upon during the long hours of her sleepless night. At whatever cost, she would continue to maintain her own integrity. And she would die rather than cast a shadow upon Nancy's happiness.

The next two days passed quickly, hastened by the ship's rapid approach upon New York. The passage had been especially favourable, and they hoped to sight the Nantucket lightship by Friday morning. Coincident with this presage of the end of the voyage, a heightening of social activity occurred, to which, saved by her pronouncement that she must rest, Katharine maintained her attitude of friendly reserve. Certain parties she was obliged to attend, but on the whole she was successful in her attempt at self-effacement. Several times she caught Madden's secret, puzzled gaze upon her, yet, until the evening of the gala dinner dance, she was spared the necessity of being with him alone.

The dance, that inevitable occasion of champagne, streamers, paper hats, and all the hectic effects of carnival, had loomed before Katharine as the greatest test of her strength, a trial she could not possibly escape. It began easily enough, for during dinner she talked chiefly to the Captain and to Lady Blandwell, maintaining a wholly fictitious absorption in the nautical platitudes of the one and the egotistical prattle of the other. But when the orchestra struck up, and coloured lights flooded the pillared room, and people began to dance, the strain upon her nerves was intensified. To sit and smile, preserving a serene untroubled face in the sight of all this gaiety, was as much as she could bear. She had the awful feeling that she might in some way betray herself. This made her lose a little of her self-possession and led her into a mistake.

The old Captain asked her to dance, and, unguardedly, thinking anything better than her present inactivity, she accepted. When he had ambled pleasantly round the floor with her, he restored her to her seat. At that moment she felt Madden's eyes upon her. So far he had danced every dance with Nancy, but now he got up and asked her to dance the next with him.

For a second, which seemed longer than a year, Katharine kept her eyes upon the table, while a sickening pounding started in her pulses. "I'm not much good," she excused herself at length.

"Oh, yes, you are," he answered. "I've just seen you."

Nancy leaned across, a cigarette between her scarlet-tipped fingers. She wore a black frock, which gave her hair an even lighter sheen, and high-heeled silver shoes. She looked more finished than ever and amazingly young. She smiled complacently. "Go on, Katharine. Bear with him for my sake."

There was no escape. Katharine rose and took the floor with Madden. He placed his arm round her, and they moved off together. He held her lightly, and, though he was clearly no expert, his steps went evenly with the music's rhythm.

"Why didn't you want to dance with me?" he asked at length. His voice was natural and quiet.

Now that she was cut off from all retreat, and in his arms, that strange pounding beat like waves in her ears. She bit her lip, summoning all her courage to support her. She managed a pale smile. "I'm too old for this sort of thing."

"What nonsense!" he declared with his quiet smile. "I should say you'd hardly begun."

"Well, let's put it that I'm thinking of other things. About landing to-morrow, and business, and my future plans."

Nothing was said for a moment. The music kept up its slow, insistent beat. She felt his eyes upon her face.

"You don't seem much interested in my plans," he said at length.

"Of course I am." In her tone she tried to convey just the right shade of perfunctoriness. "You'll stop a bit in New York?"

"Yes, I'd figured on spending a few days with you and Nancy in town, showing you around a bit. Then I hoped you'd both run up to Vermont to meet my mother and some of our folks there in Graysville."

Katharine's face was troubled. "I don't know that I'll be able to come."

"I visited *your* mother," he reminded her with an odd, persuasive smile.

There was a pause between them. She felt her position keenly.

"Very well, then," she said awkwardly. "I'll try to come along."

"That's fine," he said quickly. "I'd like you to see some of our Vermont countryside. How I loved it when I went there on a vacation when I was a kid! For that matter, how I love it now!" Again he paused, then, without any alteration in his tone, quietly went on: "By the way, Katharine, what's gone wrong between you and me? It was swell before, but now it's not so good. You've shut me out. The others don't feel it, but I do. Now, all I want to say is this: Katharine, you're a grand person. I value your friendship terribly, not only because I'm marrying Nancy, but for my own sake. Can't we get right with each other again?"

For all her courage a kind of panic took hold of Katharine. She had wanted to keep away from Madden at all costs, for Nancy's sake. But now she felt suddenly that her change of manner had been obvious and unwise. Struggling between those two currents, she had a sense of blind confusion.

"You're quite mistaken." She spoke stumblingly. "I daresay I've been rather irritable lately, but it's because I've been off-colour. I haven't meant to upset our friendship."

"You mean you haven't noticed anything yourself?"

She shook her head.

"I see," he said, and paused. Then, with an almost puzzled smile: "Well, in that case there's nothing more to be done."

The music ceased, and they came back to their table. Someone had refilled Katharine's glass. She drank quickly. The champagne, tingling through her nerves, restored her. When she looked up, Madden was dancing again with Nancy, and the doctor, coming forward, claimed his turn with her. She danced afterwards with Mr Pym, who never failed to single her out for this attention, and once more with the Captain. Then, as some of the tables were breaking up, she excused herself and went to her cabin.

She could not read, and sleep seemed equally impossible. She lay battling with the hurrying procession of her thoughts which pressed upon her relentlessly, causing her to toss fitfully from side to side. Towards morning, however, she fell into a deep sleep, and when the stewardess awoke her, they were in the harbour moving quietly, with a slow panorama of New York's skyline drifting across the ports. The sight, with its tangible evidence of the journey's end, of solid land and the prospect of escape, brought back some confidence to Katharine. She dressed quickly and went on deck.

82

Above everything she was resolved to show nothing, to yield nothing, to carry through her purpose to the end.

Katharine found Madden and Nancy on the upper deck, forward, studying the exquisite clear-cut outline of the city which seemed to rise and fill the heavens in fluted tiers like a modern Acropolis. Her own calmness reassured her, gave her new confidence.

"Beautiful, isn't it?" she remarked, including Madden in her greeting. "I'm glad you gave Nancy her first sight of it like this."

"Yes, it looks a pretty good town," Nancy said. Her small face wore a look of unusual concentration. "And it's a thrill, hitting America for the first time."

"Like Columbus," Katharine suggested lightly.

"Exactly," Nancy agreed. Her eyes narrowed slightly. "Only this time America is going to discover me."

Here Mr Pym approached, suaver and more omnipotent than ever. Singling out Katharine, discreetly he murmured:

"The reporters are on board, Miss Lorimer. I thought you might care to give them a moment, as usual."

Katharine understood the purser's friendly hint, his desire to give her arrival with the Holbein a selling value. No one had better knowledge of the commerce of news than quiet Mr Pym. Turning, she watched the group of reporters advance upon her. They were mostly young men, sophisticated and business-like, with coat collars jerked up and hats jerked down.

"Morning, Miss Lorimer," remarked the foremost, touching his brim.

Katharine recognized him as Kelly of a leading evening paper.

"Glad to see you again," he said. "How's tricks? Hear you've got a swell story for us about that little piece of antique you've brought along."

Katharine nodded, preparing to advertise her miniature attractively. But at the same moment she caught sight of Nancy's face turned with a kind of eager sharpness towards the group. All at once a wave of feeling rushed over her, swept all thought of self behind her. On an impulse she said:

"I've brought something more interesting than an antique. That little picture isn't so important. And in any case it can wait. But I'd like you to meet my niece, Nancy Sherwood. She's come over to play in Bertram's new production. If you want advance copy and photographs, now's your chance to get them, for I warn you, Nancy's going to be the hit of the show."

Instantly nine pairs of eyes were switched from Katharine to Nancy, and nine hatbrims were twitched accordingly. There was a pause.

"Well, Miss Lorimer," said Mr Kelly with conviction, "I've a hunch you're talking. How about it, boys?"

While Katharine stood aside, cameras flashed, and questions were fired upon Nancy in volleys. She rose to the experience without a tremor, her smile brilliant, her attitude charmingly audacious.

"Thanks, Katharine," she breathed, when it was over, "I only wanted a start like that."

They were alongside now, and Madden turned from the rail where he had been contemplating the scene upon the dock below. For the first time that morning he addressed himself to Katharine

"Nancy has promised to have lunch with me at the Waldorf. Won't you—won't you come, too?"

Katharine managed a gesture of regret. "Business," she said with a faint, impersonal smile. "That's going to keep me moving now."

"You won't forget Vermont, though?"

"No," she had to say, "I won't forget."

They left the desk together, and presently, when Katharine had taken leave of all her friends on board, she passed quickly through the customs. Here, by accident or design, she lost Madden and Nancy, so out on West Street she hailed a taxi and drove alone to her hotel.

84

Chapter Ten

As though it were the antidote to that dragging pain which now never seemed to leave her breast, Katharine embraced the prospect of immediate work. The moment she reached the Tower Carlton, where she always had her apartment, she rang Breuget, her American manager. Breuget, restrained from meeting her at the dock only by her express wish, had been awaiting her call and declared that he would come over immediately. She had barely time to glance round the little apartment, decorated in green and gold, which had so often harboured her; to envisage once again the fascinating view, thirty storeys below, of the great canyon of Fifth Avenue; to receive Mr Lenz, the hotel manager, who presented himself with fruit, flowers, and profound expressions of delight at her return, with the additional information that an extra bedroom had been thrown on to the suite for Miss Sherwood; before Breuget burst in, his hands outstretched, his small beard quivering with a truly Gallic welcome.

Georges Breuget was a Parisian, specialist in early bijouterie and eighteenth-century watches, who had come to New York to make his fortune, failed grotesquely, and been rescued literally from starvation by Katharine.

When he had kissed her hand, discharged a great variety of compliments at her head, and at last taken a seat upon the settee, he pressed the knob of his famous stick against his lips, as though to silence his own presumptuous loquacity, and awaited her inquiries and commands.

"Well, Breuget," she said, sitting back in her chair and inspecting him soberly, "I've brought the miniature."

"Good, Miss Lorimer."

"I hope so! Tell me, now: have you put in that work on Brandt? Exactly as I wrote you?"

"It is all arranged." Breuget rolled the r's with naïve satisfaction. "Brandt is to be in New York in ten days. On Wednesday the seventh, at three o'clock, he is coming to our place to inspect the miniature. And to buy it, Miss Lorimer. You'll see. Just like that. For certain."

Katharine's lips drew in. "I hope you're right, Breuget. Anyhow, you've done well. In the meantime we'll have the miniature in the window, exclusive frame, red velvet setting, for the whole of New York to see. Let all the dealers see it, too—Ascher and the rest of them. They'll talk a lot, and all that does good. I don't want our friend Brandt to run away with the idea that it's ready to drop into his hands at his price. It's got to be our price. Do you understand, Breuget?"

"Why, yes, Miss Lorimer. Things are a little difficult at present."

"Difficult! That lets us out too lightly. Look here, old friend, you may as well realize it. If we don't sell this miniature for near enough one hundred thousand dollars, we can both start looking for two nice new jobs."

Breuget made a composite gesture with his high shoulders, sympathetic, vaguely apologetic, yet on the whole optimistic. "We'll sell it, Miss Lorimer. Then we'll go ahead again. I tell you business is beginning to look up. If only we can get past these next few weeks, we shall be in velvet."

Katharine nodded, her eyes suddenly distant and unfathomable. "Yes," she replied, "just these next few weeks, then we'll be all right."

With a powerful effort she recalled herself. She rose and threw on her hat. "Let's go and display the Holbein. By the way, you might care to see it."

Breuget took the miniature and studied it with a reverential, enraptured eye. "Beautiful, beautiful," he murmured finally.

Beside him, Katharine considered the miniature with new eyes, touched by a vague new pity. The portrait lived for her now, invested with a strangely human interest. Here, in those features which bore some resemblance to her own, lay the foretaste of an equal sadness. Here, perhaps, was a destiny of solitude and sadness which she must also follow. Insensibly Katharine felt a flowing outward of herself, as though her spirit, trembling upon the edge of light, merged with the spirit of Lucie de Quercy. It was a strange emotion, a sense of dissolving into space and time, a faint reverberation of the echoes of the past heard amidst the crashing tumult of this great city, only in the secret places of her heart.

Breuget was speaking again. "And very strange, too, Miss Lorimer; it is so remarkably like you."

Katharine made a quick gesture which concealed the stab his words gave her. She answered almost harshly: "The next one who says that, I'm going to heave a brick at him." She swung round and led the way abruptly towards the door.

They walked down the Avenue together towards the office, a little bandbox of a place sandwiched between a smart dressmaker's and a fashionable florist's. On the way, since it was after one o'clock, Katharine treated the old man to lunch; and, since no illusions lay between them on the economic situation, they went to Childs, where they each had a club sandwich with dill pickles, followed by coffee and angel cake.

Shaking off her mood, Katharine enjoyed the savoury, typically American food. The crowds of business girls about her, rushing through their midday meal, revived in her the consciousness of her own career. It stirred her, too, when they reached the office, to place the miniature in the tiny, bronze-girded window against a background of wine-coloured Genoese velvet, and to reflect how accurately this simple act epitomized her present undivided purpose.

When Ascher dropped in on a visit of inspection, she was pleased by his evident approval. He was the most expert of the New York dealers, and she saw that her purchase impressed him favourably. But later, walking back to her hotel alone, her spirits sagged, and a physical lassitude fell upon her.

Back in her apartment she found that Nancy had arrived and,

having scattered her things about her bedroom—an act known to Nancy as unpacking—was now stretched upon the couch under a reading lamp with a tea tray at her side. The sight, in all its gentle hedonism, did something towards restoring Katharine. She kicked off her shoes and pulled on slippers. Another minute and she had shed her costume and, in an old soft afternoon gown of dove-grey colour, was seated beside Nancy, pouring herself tea. She observed, with a twitch of her lips, that Nancy had contemptuously rejected the standard little muslin bag usually offered by the hotel in favour of the private blend which Katharine had brought especially from London.

"Had a good time?" she inquired cheerfully.

"Marvellous, darling." Nancy looked up from her study of the play and fixed her large, luminous eyes on Katharine. "Most successful lunch, with the most delicious oysters—blue points, I think Chris said—and a heavenly thing called squab. Then I took Chris down to the theatre. Everyone was sweet. The *Imperial* gets in next Thursday with Bertram, Paula Brent, and the others. We start rehearsals then. I'm loving New York, Katharine, and I bet you a new hat it's going to love me."

Nancy helped herself to the last macaroon and nibbled it complacently. "You haven't seen the papers, I suppose, darling? They're there on the floor beside you. Rather fun, on the whole. Half a column in most and four really marvellous photographs."

Katharine picked up the news sheets and read them carefully. "Yes, they're splendid," she remarked when she had finished. "You've hit America quite hard!"

Nancy smiled, then stretched herself like a contented kitten. "Everyone is so marvellous to me, Katharine. Chris has been such a dear all day. I'm terribly in love with him, really. You know, he wants me to marry him right away, after the opening of the show. And I rather think I must. It would be rather fun, too, if I made a hit on the first night—and I may tell you, darling, I've got an idea I'm going to have a success!—and followed it up by getting married in the real romantic style." She paused abruptly. "You like Chris, don't you, darling?"

"You know I do."

"He likes you," Nancy continued. "He likes you a lot. He talked of you at lunch to-day. He wants you to have a meal with us to-morrow or the next day in his rooms at the Waldorf."

Katharine stared at Nancy in surprise.

"Do you mean he's staying at the Waldorf?"

"Yes, darling. Why not? Oh, I know Chris likes a quiet little pub," she smiled, "but I prefer the bright lights. And I persuaded him."

"But it's frightfully expensive there." A sudden resolution took hold of Katharine. "Listen, Nancy, are you sure Chris can afford all this running around, flowers, presents, expensive hotels? If he can't, it isn't fair to demand it of him."

"He hasn't complained," Nancy answered coolly.

"Do you think he would complain? He's not that sort. I hate saying this, Nancy, but we do want to be honest about it!"

Nancy smiled her ingenuous smile. "Don't worry, darling. Chris is all right. He's what they call a big shot in Cleveland. A little bird has told Nancy. Now don't look cross. I'm not going to argue about it. I've argued enough this afternoon over this Vermont trip."

There was a silence. Nancy was clearly in her airiest, most superficial mood, a mood which Katharine always found most trying.

Katharine said eventually: "You mean Chris wants you to go down to meet his mother?"

"Yes," said Nancy with a resigned nod. "And all the uncles and forty-second cousins. And a chorus of villagers, I suppose. He's asked us to leave on Thursday. For two days or even three. Just when I'm getting all wound up to begin rehearsals. Can you imagine it? In the dead of winter, too, chucking New York for some God-forsaken spot in the country."

"Some people like the country."

"They can have it."

"You must go," Katharine said seriously. "You really must."

"Then you must come with me," pouted Nancy.

Katharine's brow gathered into lines of deep perplexity. She saw she must go, or Nancy might not go at all.

"I can't come on Thursday," she said slowly. "But if you wish, I'll follow you the next day."

"All right," Nancy rejoined with a smile. "That'll have to do. And now let's stop talking about it. Turn on the radio and let's have some snappy music."

Chapter Eleven

On Friday morning Katharine sat in the express for Vermont en route for Graysville. She was alone, since Madden and Nancy had gone up the day before, and, sunk in the cushioned upholstery of the warm Pullman, she rubbed the steamy window with her gloved fingers and let her gaze absorb the frigid landscape which breathlessly flashed past her. Outside it was bitter cold. The train rocked through the frozen countryside, on and on, faster, louder, devouring distances which still reached illimitably onward.

The day wore on. Towards evening Katharine had to change to a local. Then on again, into a red haze of sunset which saddled the bleak earth with a strange celestial glory. Half an hour later the conductor padded along the aisle.

"Graysville in five minutes, ma'am," he murmured gently.

A little rush of emotion came over Katharine—the sense of her approaching destination, mingled with anticipation, curiosity, and a certain touch of dread. Swiftly came a quick hiss of steam and a harsh grinding of brakes, then the train rumbled to a stop, and she was out on the small bare platform, the sole passenger alighting, her suitcase beside her, her cheeks whipped by the keen wind, her eyes searching the deserted station with a kind of nervous expectation.

Immediately a man detached himself from the dark background of the empty station shed and came towards her. He was elderly, sinewy, and bandy-legged, with a short leather jacket and a chauffeur's peaked cap, beneath which his weathered face wore a grin of amiable welcome.

"You'll be Miss Lorimer," he declared with a broadening of his grin. "I'm Hickey." He picked up her case. "Come along. I've got the automobile outside the depot."

She followed the little man outside the station to the car, a high green coupé of a model at least ten years old, but so marvellously preserved and spotless that its coachwork shone like lustre and its metalwork like glass. Even the tyres were pipe-clayed immaculately. Hickey's pride in the machine was apparent as he handed Katharine in, whirred the old pistons to life, and bowled sedately down Main Street. There were few people about, but for such as stamped along the sidewalk Hickey had a wave of a hand, a genial and wholly comprehensive salute.

"Ain't many folks around," he informed Katharine companionably. "Mostly gone skatin'. Season's just started, an' they're all mighty set on it. Mr Chris said to tell you 'cept for the ice they'd 'a' bin down to the depot to meet you pers'n'lly."

"Is the skating good?" asked Katharine, half-smiling in return.

"Sure," answered the old man with his friendly tobacco-stained grin. "If it ain't, it ought to be. Theer's thirty mile of lake froze' here."

As though to point his remark he drew up the car at this juncture and with vigorous pantomime invited a couple marching ahead with their skates, who laughingly hailed him, to clamber into the rumble seat. They were a girl and her brother, second cousins of the Maddens, Hickey confided to Katharine as they started off again. There seemed, indeed, no limit to the old fellow's encyclopedic garrulity. While he ran on, with the privilege of an old servant who is also a local character and knows it, Katharine, listening amusedly, nevertheless found time to study the prospect of the wintry yet homely scene. The road, leaving the town behind, struck down to the lake, a lovely stretch of icebound water, and wound along its shores, fringed with willow and juniper. Far off a ridge of hills rose into the gathering dusk. The ring of skates was borne distantly. And already, floating out of the east, came a pale disc of moon.

Something of the strange enchantment of the moment and the

place entered into Katharine and sang mysteriously in her blood. She was silent as, with much banter and explosive guffaws and reminders not to be late for supper, old Hickey discharged his extra passengers at a little landing stage beside a private boatshed, then turned the nose of the coupé towards a white house which stood at the end of its drive amid an orchard of twisted apple trees. It was a simple, unassuming place, an old Colonial frame house with a plain Georgian façade. A moment later and the car had crunched to rest, and the door was flung open. Then Katharine was in the hall shaking hands with Mrs Madden herself.

She knew at once it was Chris's mother, the resemblance was so marked in this tall and gaunt-framed woman. Her face had the same repose as Madden's. She suggested an equal calmness, and a certain constancy, as though the discipline of her life had bred in her patience, fortitude, and gentleness. Her eyes, which had a curious quality of depth, were fixed on Katharine warmly, hospitably.

"You must be frozen," she said when the ordinary greetings were exchanged. "Come and thaw out in your room."

She turned and showed Katharine upstairs to a front bedroom where a vigorous fire blazed and crackled in an open Dutch stove, throwing a cheerful leaping glow upon the fourposter bed, the fine lace curtains, the heavy fruit-wood chest and solid chairs.

"I hope you'll be comfortable here," said Mrs Madden with a sudden shyness which went straight to Katharine's heart. "It's very plain. But then we're plain people."

"It's lovely—lovely," Katharine answered impulsively.

Mrs Madden smiled, a slow reserved smile which cast a kind of radiance upon her austere features. She seemed to search for words expressive of her satisfaction, but it was clear words did not come easily to her. She lingered for a moment by the doorway, seeing that everything was at Katharine's hand, then, observing that supper would be served presently, she quietly departed.

Thirty minutes later Katharine went downstairs into the parlour, a long, brightly lit room which opened off the hall, and was now filled most unexpectedly with people. The skating party had returned, bringing with them a great many friends and village folks. It was Katharine's first intimation of the open hospitality kept at Lakeside House.

Madden and Nancy stood by the fire with the laughing couple who had travelled in the rumble seat and who were now presented as Luke and Betty Lou. Beside them, sitting bolt upright in his rocker, was an old man with a wrinkled, humorous face. Uncle Ben Emmet, Mrs Madden's brother. Opposite sat the Graysville schoolmaster and his sister. Then came Doc Edwards, short and shabby in a thick pilot coat; Pop Walters, fat, bald-headed, his eye shrewd and twinkling. Afterward, Sammy Emmet, Ben's grandson, with a freckled nose and, like Luke, a college fraternity pin on his vest. And a score of others, young men and women in bright sweaters, cheeks and eyes burnished by the wind, laughing and talking at the end of the room.

It took Katharine some time to get around this large assembly, but, sponsored by Mrs Madden, who took the matter with an anxious gravity, she was duly introduced to everyone at last. There was nothing remarkable about the gathering, composed of ordinary and, in some instances, humble-looking people who looked as though they worked hard for a living. Yet each had a quality of open and unstudied friendliness, more disarming than all the manners in the world. Immediately, Katharine felt at home.

She had no chance to say much to Nancy or Chris, for Mrs Madden took her arm, and the whole party went in to supper at once.

Katharine, hungry from her long journey and the keen air, ate with a good appetite. Among so many it was impossible to concentrate upon her personal reactions. Madden, in a dark grey polo sweater, was at the foot of the table carving steadily. Nancy, halfway down, wore an air that was almost remote. Fork in one hand, cigarette in the other, she was smoking as she ate, barely listening to the conversation of Sammy Emmet upon her right. Instinctively Katharine's brow gathered in perplexity. But her immediate neighbours, Walters and the Little Doc Edwards, gave her no time for reflection.

"You try some of this elderberry wine, Miss Lorimer," Doc Edwards bent forward earnestly. "It's all home-made by Susan Madden. I'll promise you it keeps the cold out."

Katharine tried the well-spiced wine and agreed that it was excellent. She smiled at the little man.

"You ought to take some on your rounds with you. It must be hard work getting about the country this bitter weather."

He stared at her, round-eyed, then broke into genial noiseless merriment. "You got me wrong," he intimated at last. "The folks just call me Doc. I ain't that much of a medico. I only keep that no-account drugstore on the corner of Main Street by the Baptist Church."

Katharine dropped her eyes, a trifle confused to have mistaken the social status of her neighbour. But he went on, quite undisturbed, in the same modest, friendly style.

"We ain't a stuck-up lot in these parts, ma'am. Though Chris Madden has got on so fine, he ain't forgot Joe Edwards was the one that took him fishing when he warn't no more than seven year old."

"Did you?" asked Katharine with quick interest.

"Sure I did. When Chris come up to his Uncle Ben's on the summer vacation. An' I reckon Susan was hard enough put to it to find his railroad fare those days. But what's the odds? Out we went trollin' on the lake, an', by George! you oughta seen that boy's face when he pulled out his first big bass."

Katharine had a swift picture of the scene, the sun-bleached boat idling on the rippling lake, the bent hickory rod, the silver fish flopping on the centreboard, and Chris's childish face, flushed, wildly excited, yet curiously intent. She was silent. She saw vividly the tie which bound Madden to his mother's native place. She understood why he was known, respected, loved. Grown up now and successful though he was, he was still Susan Emmet's boy in Graysville.

When supper was over, they went back into the parlour. A sedate bridge four was established at one table and at the other a wild round game which went by the name of Animal Crackers. Katharine was invited by young Sammy Emmet to roast chestnuts on the fire bars.

She sat on the hearthrug, with the cheerful gaiety of the room about her. The fun at the round table, where Madden was the centre of the game, waxed fast and furious. Once or twice it struck her that Chris's voice held a note of gaiety almost forced. But she could not be sure, and the heat of the fire was making her drowsy now, deliciously tired. Half an hour later she said good-night quietly to Mrs Madden and slipped up to her room.

She had not long been there before Nancy joined her, drifting in with the inevitable cigarette between her lips.

"Glad to escape?" she inquired casually.

"Escape from what?" asked Katharine in surprise.

Nancy did not answer. But she gave a little nervous shrug.

"Nancy!" exclaimed Katharine directly. "Don't you like it here?"

Nancy raised her brows slightly. "It's very nice, darling. A little comic, perhaps."

"Comic?" echoed Katharine bluntly.

Nancy nodded. She saw that Katharine did not grasp her mood, and this suddenly made her hard. She drawled:

"Too many antimacassars about, darling. And poor relations eating hard and laughing at everything. And giggling village maidens, and texts, like that one there, above the beds."

Katharine's eyes followed Nancy's to the framed square of needlework upon the wall.

"That isn't a text," she said briefly. "It's a sampler, and it's most beautifully stitched."

"Well, anyhow," Nancy said with a sudden burst of nerves, "it isn't my cup of tea. A week of this place would drive me frantic. I feel they're suspicious of me here because I'm on the stage. Every time I light a cigarette they look at me as if I were committing the unpardonable sin. There isn't even a decent movie show in the wretched little hick town. Why couldn't Chris have produced his dumb relations in Cleveland if he had to inflict them on us? Thank heaven we're leaving for New York the day after to-morrow."

"Nancy!"

"Oh, I'm sorry, Katharine!" Nancy relented instantly. Her mouth drooped, and she stood, her wide eyes full of genuine contrition. "I know I'm jumpy and unsatisfactory just now. I shouldn't have come here till after the show. I'm sorry for Chris's sake. But at the moment I'm right out of tune. I'm keyed up for something quite different."

"For what?"

"For the play, of course. Oh, don't you see, Katharine, how much it means to me, how much I want success? I've got Chris, I know, and I'm happy, terribly happy with him. But I want the other thing as well, success in my career, oh, terrific success!"

Katharine was silent, almost staggered by the intensity in Nancy's voice. For the first time she saw exactly the height and strength of Nancy's ambition. A slow wave of dismay crept over her. Nancy wanted fame. But had she the quality to win it? Beauty, intelligence, and talent she had, of course. But the other elusive quality, the depth and maturity of character which alone can make an actress great, had Nancy that? Suddenly Katharine was afraid, most terribly afraid for Nancy.

"Don't you think you're demanding rather a lot from life?" she asked in a low voice.

"Perhaps," Nancy nodded. "But oh, Katharine, I mean to have it."

Coming forward she kissed Katharine good-night, and in a moment she had left the room.

Katharine remained standing by the window, her figure motionless, her lips compressed. Outside was the still beauty of the night, around her lay the peace of this quiet and unspoiled community. She had an impulse to go to Nancy, to speak to her, comfort her, restrain her. But she held herself back, feeling it would be unwise. She felt herself both baffled and anxious. She sighed and went silently to bed.

Chapter Twelve

Katharine was awakened next morning by bright sunshine in her room and the sound of much activity within the house and without. Something in the brisk and bustling alacrity uplifted her heart. She jumped out of bed, dressed quickly in a warm tweed suit, and went down to the breakfast room, where Mrs Madden, Chris, Uncle Ben, and young Sammy Emmet were on the point of sitting down to breakfast.

"Why," said Mrs Madden, half-rising, her face lighting up, "we didn't think you'd want to come down for breakfast. Nancy likes to have her tray later in bed."

Katharine smiled. "I want to get out, a morning like this. Especially if there's skating ahead."

"Spoken like a man," cried Sammy, thumping a hot doughnut on his plate. "You'll come out with young Emmet himself, for that!"

Katharine took her place, accepting the hot coffee which Mrs Madden poured for her, and the broiled ham which Chris served from the pewter platter in front of him. The doughnuts, recommended by Sammy as Mrs Hickey's chef d'oeuvre, were crisp and light. It was a happy meal for Katharine. As at supper on the night before, she felt again that atmosphere of candour and unaffected cheerfulness which had so deeply touched her. She could not but see, too, that the simple fact of her joining the family at this early breakfast had given Chris's mother deep and unconcealed pleasure.

Immediately afterward they started for the lake. Sammy, who had clearly made Katharine his own affair, would brook no delay, and although there was as yet no sign of Nancy, he rooted out a nice pair of skates from the woodshed and marched her off towards the ice. Madden came with them as far as the landing stage.

It was a delicious morning. As she walked down the hard road between Sammy and Madden, Katharine could have wished the path an endless one. Everyone they met knew Chris and gave him a quick, spontaneous greeting of friendship and respect. Now, with her impressions of the night before, she had a perfect insight of his real character, his true value, that balance of sympathy and strength which caused him never to forsake his household gods and never to forget a friend.

At the boathouse Sammy, kneeling with much exuberance and ardour, fitted on her skates. Then they were off, the pair of them, skimming over the glassy surface like birds upon the wing. Madden, standing immobile on the landing stage, watched them vanish round the bend of the creek. His face wore a curious expression. He loved skating and had not had much of it in these last years. He might have wished himself free to go with them, to get on the ice at once. Perhaps it was this which caused his eyes to wear a queer perplexity as he turned and made his way slowly back towards the house to wait for Nancy.

It was nearly half-past two before Katharine and Sammy returned. Lunch, apparently, was over, the table cleared of food and the house of people, but when they burst in, brimming with laughter and apology, Mrs Madden gave an understanding inclination of her head.

"Don't make a fuss," she smiled. "I saved everything for you in the oven."

Within five minutes she had paid a stately visit to the kitchen, the tablecloth was replaced; then she sat, watching them eat, as though she drew a quiet satisfaction from the obvious appeasement of their hunger.

"Are you skating again this afternoon?" Mrs Madden asked at length.

Katharine shook her head. "I feel as if I had no ankles left. And

Chris said something about going out after supper. All of us. They're lighting a bonfire on one of the islands. This afternoon I ought to rest."

The old woman hesitated. "Would you take a cup of coffee with me? I often have one by the fire about three."

In the parlour it was quiet and oddly subdued. The eightday clock ticked solemnly in the corner, and the lustres on the walnut tallboy winked and flickered in the firelight. Sammy had departed, whistling, to inspect a litter of puppies which Hickey and he were raising in the barn. Mrs Madden, having poured the coffee, said nothing for a long time. At last however, she moved and, with her eyes averted, remarked:

"I'm glad you came here, Katharine. Now I've got on a bit in years, I daresay I don't take much to people. But when I do, it means a lot to me."

Katharine, both touched and embarrassed, made no reply. And in a moment, inconsequently, Mrs Madden reached out her hand and picked a plush-covered album from the nearby table. It was a family album, an object both grave and ludicrous, a queer survival of the past which would, Katharine involuntarily reflected, have instantly set Nancy's teeth on edge. But there was nothing to take exception to in Mrs Madden's voice as she went on:

"There's a likeness of Chris here. It's quite a good one."

Katharine accepted the open album, her gaze falling upon a faded yellow photograph of a little boy, not more than seven, in short pants, and a ridiculous old straw hat turned up from his brow. Yes, it was Chris. She would have known at any age those dark eyes that glanced towards her from the childish face with such a serious inquiry. Her breast contracted with tenderness. By a great effort she conquered the rush of foolish tears that sprang instinctively beneath her lowered lashes.

"It's a lovely little photograph," she said. "You must show it to Nancy."

"I have," said Chris's mother slowly.

Katharine looked up quickly, then quickly looked away again.

She had surprised in the other woman's eyes a troubled look that cut her to the heart.

"It's stupid of me to say it," Mrs Madden went on even more slowly, "but I'd like my Chris to be happy."

"He will be," said Katharine.

"Nancy's mighty sweet." Mrs Madden hesitated. "Yet somehow I can't get used to her being on the stage. Old-fashioned, I reckon."

"She'll settle down all right." Katharine spoke warmly.

"We got talking about that the other night," mused Mrs Madden. "Somehow it cropped up. Before you came. And Nancy seems to be figuring on keeping on with the stage after she marries Chris. She made quite a little speech about it. Got all worked up. Said nowadays a girl could be married and have a career as well. In my young days being married was a girl's career. But I guess it's different these modern times. We must be reasonable. I like Nancy a lot. I only want her and my Chris to be happy."

"They will be," said Katharine impulsively. "I know Nancy. She's very young, but she's fine all through. And I don't honestly believe she'll want to go on with the stage much longer. At least. . ." she paused, remembering her premonitions of Nancy's ultimate disappointment, "when Nancy finds she can't be a star, she'll settle down and be a wife. If we let things alone, they're bound to straighten themselves out."

"I hope so. I hope so!" repeated Mrs Madden with that quiet gravity in her thoughtful eyes.

The entry of Mrs Hickey with a plate of fresh-baked biscuits interrupted the conversation. And thereafter neither Katharine nor Susan Madden resumed it.

Katharine did not go out that afternoon. She judged that the expedition arranged for the evening would prove sufficiently exciting. Indeed, when suppertime came, an even larger party arrived than on the night before. But there was no time wasted at table. They were all eager to get away. And so about eight o'clock a score or more of them went down from the house towards the lake. Madden was there, but Nancy had refused to come, vowing, pleasantly enough, that if anyone showed her a skate again, she would go crazy. In any case, she added, she was going to her room to work.

At the boathouse, when skates had been adjusted, they all set off under the sparkling radiance of the sky, with arms crossed and hands linked, swinging down the ice in one long human chain. The motion, combined and rhythmic, blended insensibly with the ecstasy of the night. Above them the moon, like a great lantern hung high in the heavens, cast its light upon the frozen waters. To the south the snug rooftops of the village lay glittering with frost. To the east the mountains made a ridge that might have been the threshold of the gods. In front lay the lovely stretch of ice, dark yet luminous, polished as marble, smooth as agate, reaching forward, forward out into the bay.

Breathlessly, Katharine swung onward. Often at home she had skated upon the tiny ponds around London, in gloomy fog or threatening thaw. But never had she known such a glorious expanse, such splendid air, such virgin ice as this. Her heart soared. The ring of the skates made music in her ears. The wind, whipping her cheeks, sending her scarf ends sailing, sent the blood coursing in her veins more madly than champagne.

They reached the island at last, a little round hummock of dry spruce and bush willow five miles down the lake, and there, in a few minutes, the bonfire prepared beforehand was sent leaping into life. As the flames went sparkling upward, the skaters gathered round in a wide circle. Vacuum flasks were unscrewed, and hot milk and coffee passed from hand to hand. Betty Lou, unearthing treasure, produced a bag of ginger cookies from her sealskin muff. Then Andy Dunn, the clerk at the village store, unslung the accordion from his shoulder and began unobtrusively to play. He played the old familiar tunes, tenderly, dreamily—'Swanee River', 'Aunt Dinah's Quilting Party', 'Uncle Ned'—the thin sweet melody rising heavenward towards the stars. Before they knew it, they were singing.

Katharine glanced round the circle, at the happy singing faces lit by the firelight, and for the second time that day a tear of genuine emotion trembled upon her eye. She wished with all her heart that Nancy had come. There was within this ring a tacit admission of affection, of that common brotherhood which bound all humanity upon the earth.

And now they swung into the loveliest tune of all, 'Juanita'. Katharine could not help herself. Her soul was drawn from her, she was one with this company now. She joined in the song.

Glancing suddenly at Madden as she sang, she caught his eyes upon her. All that day—indeed, since her arrival—she had scarcely seen him. But now something queer and almost startled in his look caught her unawares. He was staring at her as though seeing her dimly, or strangely, or for the first time in his life.

When the song finished, there was a long pause, then, as if realizing that nothing more could now be sung, they rose with a burst of chatter. Immediately Katharine was conscious of Madden at her elbow. He spoke in a voice that seemed oddly strained.

"It was nice of you to join with us like that." "Why not?" She laughed a little uncomfortably. "Even if I can't sing a note."

"What does that matter?" he replied. "It was just the way you did it."

When they linked arms to go home, Madden was still by her side. His hand in its coarse woollen glove clasped hers lightly. He scarcely spoke during their return up the lake, and when they reached the house, he stole a quick glance at her, then bade her good-night in that same suppressed tone.

But he did not go directly to bed. Leaving the others, he strode out into the orchard where the moon made strange distorted shadows amongst the apple-trees. He stood for a moment as though bewildered. In an absent, fumbling fashion he tried to light his pipe. But the pipe went out and was clenched, unheeded, by his teeth. Then a light sprang suddenly to being in Katharine's curtained window. It seemed to bring equal enlightenment to Madden. He stared at it dumbly, then, turning, he pressed his brow against the cold bark of a knotted branch. His face, caught in that pallid light, was distorted as the shadows of the orchard trees.

Chapter Thirteen

Back in New York again. It was only Monday, and yet, for Katharine, ages seemed to have passed since she had stepped into Grand Central Station three days before. Surrounded by the tumult of the city, the whole experience of her visit to Graysville became remote and intangible as a lovely dream.

Nancy and Madden had come down, too, since Bertram had arrived on the *Imperial,* and rehearsals had begun at once. Madden intended going on to Cleveland later, but meanwhile, at Nancy's behest, he was again at the Waldorf.

During the ensuing days Katharine saw nothing of him, and, indeed, she had little enough of Nancy's society. Now Madden seemed the exemplar of devotion, for although Nancy was obliged to spend most of her day at the theatre, he was continually on hand, ready to escort her for lunch, tea, or dinner to such of the exclusive restaurants as her whim demanded. Nancy, restored to sophistication, plunged enthusiastically into work. Yet though she was so busy she somehow managed to enjoy her return to city life. Arranging ahead, she made a date for Thursday, when she, Madden, and Katharine would go to a night club.

Katharine, on her part, had no inclination to go, but she yielded to Nancy's whim. Meanwhile she tried hard to concentrate her activities exclusively upon business. She thought a great deal of the miniature, waiting with increasing tension for Brandt's arrival.

It was, she told herself, this atmosphere of uncertainty which played upon her nerves. When Thursday came, her mood was unsettled, and she felt jumpy and overstrung. Only one thing was clear—deep yet unacknowledged, her longing with all her heart to see Madden again.

But when she did see him on Thursday she was startled by the change in him. He seemed thinner, older, and there were black shadows beneath his eyes.

It was a strange meeting. All their intervening friendship, the memory of those intimate days in London and during the early part of the crossing, of that recent night when they had skated back across the lake at Graysville, seemed to have slipped away from him. His manner was constrained, almost painfully detached. He did not look at her. His hand, when she took it, was cold. For Katharine it was a cruel moment. Nancy, wrapped in herself, noticed nothing.

They stood for a few minutes in the lobby of the hotel. Talk went haltingly. And then, as though striving to ease the situation, Madden led the way outside to a taxi. The night club was crowded when they arrived, but they found an especially good table reserved for them. Again Katharine, holding the image of Madden in his dark sweater, a simple person amongst simple country folk, was confounded by the brevity with which he secured the best in service and attention. He seemed different, harder than before. He ordered champagne, a magnum.

Despite the champagne, once again conversation languished. Fortunately almost immediately the lights were lowered, and the first part of the cabaret began. Daisy Jervis was the star. Caught by the spotlight, she came forward to the microphone in the middle of the floor and began her first number. She was a famous radio and cabaret performer— not beautiful, yet she had intense vitality, a personality which came over like the kick of a mule.

Nancy listened attentively, her professional faculties critically alert. But Katharine, though compelled by something in the strident rhythm of the song, could not take her eyes from Madden's profile, which in this light appeared thinner and more harassed than before. She could not understand the change in him. He was smoking incessantly, and his restless fingers were yellow with nicotine. She had never noticed this before. Was it evidence of the secret strain which seemed by some mysterious mischance suddenly to have possessed him? He continued to avoid her eyes. His lips were pinched, the set of his jaw was fixed and sombre.

The number finished, Nancy, still oblivious of anything unusual, sipped her champagne and commented upon their neighbours. Already Nancy was familiar with most of the social figures about town, and her remarks, thrown out with a slightly patronizing air, made a satiric monologue which might, in other circumstances, have been amusing. Suddenly she waved her hand, recognizing a party from the cast of *Dilemma* in a far corner.

"There's Bertram over there, Katharine," she murmured. "With the Brent woman and John Sidney. Bertie hasn't got as good a table as we have. One up for you, Chris."

Daisy Jervis began her next song, a tough Broadway number full of sharp dissonance and sudden raucous melody. It was the hit of the moment, and everyone stopped talking, drinking, and eating to listen. The voice, brazenly amplified, held the rush and clamour of the streets, the hard glitter of modern life, its harshness, carelessness, deceit.

Katharine listened with the rest; there was no escape from that strident, throbbing rhythm. But the thing hurt her, made her sick at heart. She glanced around the heated, luxurious room, crammed with flowers, jewels, money, rich exotic foods and wines, and with humanity, scented, oiled, bedecked in silks and shirt fronts, the men with sly, hard faces, the women beautiful, painted, metallic.

A wave of hopelessness came upon Katharine and with it an oppressed desire for escape. She thought of Graysville, and the lovely Vermont countryside, of all the simplicities that life could offer: fresh air, plain food, and the clean sweet breath of the open country. And a painful longing, such as she had never known, came upon her to be done with artifice and to seek the ultimate realities of life in austerity and repose. It was, she reflected with sudden retrospective insight, such a longing as might have taken poor Lucie de Quercy when, returning from the worldliness of the Tudor court, she found her lover dead and her happiness destroyed.

The lights went up. Katharine could not see Madden's face, which was shielded by his hand, but Nancy gave a gasp of pleasure.

"She's good! She's got something. And it was a cracking number!"

Katharine took a long draught of ice water. Nancy's remark jarred upon her. The surrounding scene became more shallow and more futile. And then, to her relief, an attendant approached and delivered the message that Miss Lorimer was wanted on the phone. Excusing herself, Katharine rose and followed the man out.

A queer silence ensued when Nancy and Madden were left alone.

"Katharine doesn't seem quite herself to-night," said Nancy at length. "But, after all, this isn't quite her style."

Madden was making patterns with his fork upon the tablecloth, but now he roused himself. "No," he said, "it isn't."

"Poor Katharine!" said Nancy. "She does her best!"

He threw a quick glance at her. "She's done a fair amount for you, hasn't she?"

"Oh, yes," Nancy returned lightly, "of course she has. And if I may say so, darling, she loves doing it!"

Madden took himself in hand. He lifted his head, poured himself out another full glass of champagne, and drank it, then leaned across the table. "Look here, Nancy," he said in a steady tone, "I've got something important to say to you. I've been thinking it over ever since we left Graysville. We're going to get married, you and I, at once."

"Well, aren't we?" Nancy laughed lightly.

"Yes." His dark eyes remained sombrely on hers. "But you'll notice I said at once. It must be definite between us now. All settled for the end of next week."

"Why, Chris!"

"Why not?" he insisted in a firm voice. "You love me, don't you?"

"You know I do."

"Then it's settled. A week from Saturday. When I come back from Cleveland and you get through with the opening of the show."

Moved and flattered by the intensity of his words, Nancy's eyes fell. "All right," she whispered. "It's settled, darling." She added:

"And really I'm frightfully glad. You know, I had an awful feeling in Graysville that you'd ask me to give up the stage before we got married."

"Did you?"

She nodded. "My fault, perhaps, but I did feel a little out of sympathy up there. I felt all the time your folks were grudging me my career. And it means so much to me, darling." Her eyes were tender now and luminous with a genuine emotion. "Oh, I realize I haven't done much yet. But I will, I will! And not stupid parts in stupid plays, but the real thing—Ibsen and Shaw and Shakespeare. I'll play Ophelia some day, Chris, so that you'll hold your breath. I know I can do it. I must do it. I'll make you proud of me. It's awful, darling, to have such a compulsion in one's blood. It's like loving you. I can't help it. I can't give it up. And why should I give it up? We're two clever people in love. And we're living in the twentieth century. There's no reason under the sun why I shouldn't have you and yet have my career as well. Is there, darling, is there?"

Her plea, so unexpected and sincere, moved him unaccountably. His eyes were hidden, but he reached across and pressed her hand. His voice was full of sympathy as he answered:

"I didn't understand at first, Nancy, but I guess I do now. I thought you were just fooling around in the theatre. Now I know I was wrong. And believe me, if it doesn't make any difference to you, then it doesn't to me either."

There was a silence.

"People have always fought over this question of marriage and career. But we'll solve it, won't we, Chris?"

"Yes, we'll solve it."

"Thanks, Chris," she whispered. "That makes me love you all the more." Another pause, then: "And you, darling? You do love me an awful lot, too?"

His gaze lifted towards hers with that level, unwavering regard. "Yes," he answered, "I do love you, Nancy. Haven't I told you so a hundred times?"

When Katharine returned, they were talking normally. It was

quite late. The band was playing with that bright animation which presages the moment of its release. Madden glanced at her directly for the first time in the evening. He seemed at last to be at ease, and his tone was quietly pleasant.

"Good news, I hope?"

Katharine smiled faintly. "It was Breuget on the wire. Brandt just called him from Chicago, definitely confirming arrangements. He's just had the photographs I sent him— the coloured enlargements of the Holbein—and he's fallen hard. He's flying to New York to-morrow and meeting me at three. All I have to do now is put the miniature in his hands, and it's sold."

"Smart work!" Nancy tapped her applause upon the table. Her face was brilliant with her own happiness. "Congratulations, darling! I'm so glad."

"That's something off your mind," Madden added. "Yes," Katharine said. "It is."

The band was now at its final number. The time was two o'clock. People were leaving.

"Well," said Madden, "I guess we all ought to be in bed."

Nancy laughed gaily. "Nonsense, darling! Much too early. We haven't done celebrating." Rising, she pulled her wrap about her. "We'll join up with Bertram's party and go along to Longchamps for a sandwich."

A shadow came over Madden's tired face and was as quickly suppressed. Somehow Katharine sensed that he had no wish to prolong the evening. But though he made as if to speak, he did not. In the lobby outside they met Bertram and the others. Leslie Jean Marks and Gloria Bishop somehow got mixed into the party, too, and the gilt mirrors on the walls magnified their numbers and made the scene important enough, even for Nancy. Afterwards Katharine, had she wished it, had no chance to talk to Madden again. The next day, as he had planned, he left for Cleveland.

Chapter Fourteen

Towards three o'clock on the following afternoon Katharine went down to her office to keep her appointment with Brandt. A thin rain permeated the air, oozing from the blanket of raw vapour that hung overhead. Contrary to her custom, Katharine took a taxi, and as she slid along in the cab the texture of her consciousness seemed as grey and confusedly impenetrable as those swathes of fog outside. Memories of the night before—the night club, Daisy Jervis, the party at Longchamps, Nancy's gaiety, and Madden's stoic face—all whirled giddily inside her head.

And she thought, more soberly, of Madden's return to Cleveland, of how, shedding the unaccustomed leisure of these last weeks, he would revert to another level of existence, mundane and practical, befitting his real position. She saw him stepping from the train, grip in hand, coat collar up and hat pulled down, his dark, serious, face turned in the direction of his business, a small one-chimneyed factory, where his staff, manager, foreman, stenographer, and perhaps half a hundred hands would turn out loyally to welcome him. How her concept rose she could not tell, yet she was convinced of its reality, as though the scene were now enacted before her eyes.

She sighed and took a firmer grasp of her all too sensitive emotions, facing the prospect of the immediate interview with Brandt with all the vigour she could command. Once she had sold the miniature she could make her plans for a quick return to England. Nancy's opening night—then there was nothing to keep her. Madden and Nancy would not want her any longer. She would be of small use to them, she reflected bitterly, upon their honeymoon.

A shiver went over her as she stepped out of the cab and passed quickly through the raw air. Breuget was waiting for her in the back office, a tiny cubbyhole with barely room for a desk, an electric grill, and a couple of chairs. He was nervous, she saw at once, though his lean form and aquiline features were strung to a pretence of polite unconcern. And with an air absurdly and pathetically festive he had brewed some coffee on his little stove which, with a plate of sweet biscuits, he now offered her by way of celebration and refreshment.

Katharine accepted. It was good coffee, hot and strong, with the real French tang. As she drank it she studied the old man—his lined, sensitive face, his suit, shiny from repeated pressings and worn at the cuffs, his linen, spotless yet suspiciously threadbare, with a careful darn just beneath the high stiff collar, his shoes, so meticulously polished that the the tiny cracks in the uppers hardly showed—and all at once an immense compassion awoke in her. She had never given much attention to Breuget before, except to consider the usefulness of this spinsterly old gentleman to her, but now she read him with a new sympathy, seeing his fight against shabbiness, the whole deprecatory struggle for genteel existence.

"By the way," she remarked suddenly, "if we put this deal across, we're going to raise your salary."

Breuget coloured to the roots of his sparse grey hair. "Oh, no, Miss Lorimer."

"Oh, yes, Breuget," she answered decisively.

He glanced at her, doglike, then looked away. "Thank you, Miss Lorimer," he stammered. "Thank you very much."

There was a silence. He looked at his watch, a thin gold-and-enamel Louis Philippe timepiece, relic of his former standing. "I wish Mr Brandt would come."

"It isn't three yet, surely?"

"Just, Miss Lorimer."

"Don't fidget, Breuget." Her eyes smiled at him kindly, confidently, attributing his nervousness to a new cause. "That raise is in your pocket already."

He said hurriedly: "It isn't that I'm thinking of. It's you, Miss

Lorimer. After all, it's pretty important. . ." He broke off with a wan shrug.

"Brandt'll take it." She spoke conclusively. "After what he said. We know him, don't we? He keeps his word."

Again a silence fell, which they filled, both of them, by thinking of their famous client. Brandt was, as Katharine had declared, a man who knew what he wanted and had always got it, a short, dark, thickset figure with bespectacled yet piercing eyes, who had battled his way to fabulous wealth through the twin interests of transport and lumber. His name was a national axiom for achievement. The tale of his creations—from the great chain of lumber camps he had made in the Northwest to the new biochemical institute he had founded for humanity at San Francisco—had become almost legendary, and the computation of his treasures, which filled his castle in Spain, his palazzo in Venice, and his great baroque house near Key West, a harmonic progression in millions.

Merely to think of him brought him in person to the room, so vivid was his personality, and it was with a start that Katharine emerged from her reverie to find herself still alone with Breuget, whose watch, ticking relentlessly, showed a quarter past three.

"Queer, Miss Lorimer, isn't it?" said the old man, clearing his throat. "Shall I . . . shall I ring up his house?"

Katharine made a gesture of dissent. "We mustn't worry him. He'll be along all right, unless he's been held up. In that case they'd ring us."

"Yes, Miss Lorimer."

But the suspense, with all that it implied, was proving too much for Breuget. Detaching himself from his seat, he sidled imperceptibly into the front office, and, in an attitude of expectation, took up his position behind the narrow glass door, where his eye could command the section of sidewalk directly in front.

Katharine, resting her cheek upon her palm, continued to wait, her ear, attuned to catch the door's opening click, hearing only the roar of the traffic and the shrill calling of a newsboy outside. It came to her eventually that this calling was unusually shrill and feverish. But at the same instant Breuget burst back upon her with a paper in his hand, his aspect so disordered she thought he must have had a stroke. At first he could not speak. He stood upon the threshold swaying slightly, his eyes wild, his face chalky except for a high spot of colour on his cheekbones. At last he stammered:

"Look, Miss Lorimer! Look!"

She jumped up, torn by a sudden fear. "What is it?"

"Brandt—he's—he won't buy the miniature after all." He choked out the words, his face distorted now, then, sinking into a chair, he began unashamedly to weep.

Katharine tore open the paper he had given her, and there, sprawled in black headlines across the entire page, was the news of the aeroplane disaster which had plunged Brandt and ten others to their deaths.

Chapter Fifteen

Katharine walked out of the office into the thickening mist as though her one desire now were to bury herself from human sight and contact. With head erect and eyes that stared unseeingly before her, she marched down Sixty-first Street, across Madison, and arrived by a kind of dumb instinct at the open and deserted oasis of Central Park. After walking about for a few minutes, she sat down upon a bench beside the frozen lake and strove blindly to compose her thoughts.

At first nothing reached her but the dull horror of Brandt's sudden end. She had liked the man. In all his dealings with her he had been scrupulously just, revealing through the aura of his powers a character in essence so simple and magnanimous that she had come to regard him not only as her patron, but as her friend. And now he was gone.

Desolation rushed upon her as she sat, a strange, solitary figure, in the forsaken park. Around her in the enshrouding gloom rose the minarets and temples of a great civilization humming with the note of multitudinous life. Yet here she was alone. Upon the icy pond before her some children had been skating, but they were long gone home, leaving only the churned rime of their skate tracks. A few water fowl, their cold wings folded over stilted legs, brooded disconsolately in the shelter of the little island. The park lamps strung like blurred beads upon an invisible chain stretched into nothingness. The rest was gloom and muffled silence.

Gradually her own position dawned upon her. She was finished. With Brandt so tragically removed, her chances of disposing of the miniature speedily and favourably had vanished to all but an infinitesimal point of chance. Her commitments to the bank would shortly fall due. To meet them and her other obligations, she must sell out—if indeed they did not sell her out—everything she possessed: stock, lease, even the good will of the business itself. With luck she might shave the ignominious edge of bankruptcy. But, with or without such luck, she was down, beaten, ruined. This was the end of her career, the pitiful downfall of that house of cards she had built by her utmost endeavour. A pang transfixed her at the thought of her early flashing hopes, all brutally extinguished now, of her sweet transient success, all turned to ashes in her mouth.

Then, with a swift evolution of her pain, she thought of those whom her failure would involve. Walters and Miss Mills, Breuget—alas for poor Breuget!—and, above all, her mother would feel the shock of her collapse. Nancy, thank God, did not need her now. But the others—oh, it was too crushing to contemplate, that they must suffer because of her. She could still work, of course, and driven by that relentless, conscientious strain, direct inheritance from her puritanical father, she might well slave herself into a premature old age. But could she ever attain the affluence she had previously known? Others, and she thought of Bertram, might gaily lose and then re-make a fortune in a year. But she was different. The orbit of her star was measured rather than erratic. When it fell, it would plunge never to rise again. Besides, she had felt herself strangely defenceless lately, and vulnerable to the tear and turbulence of life. Now, indeed, at this moment, she was supremely and agonizingly conscious of her sex. She was a woman, weak and helpless, needful of a sustaining arm, of a stronger will to which she might turn, and weeping, invoke protection.

All at once an impulse of despair flooded her, of such utter and abandoned hopelessness she was tempted to end the process of disaster by the swift surrender of life itself. So easy it would be to seek the dark, kind Lethe of oblivion. No one need know. One step, mistaken in the traffic—an accident, of course—and she would be out of her distress, asleep, and soon forgotten.

But in the same instant a shudder of revulsion passed over her, and she thrust away the thought as though it were unclean. Courage! That had been the motto of her life, always courage, nothing else mattered, and now she must bring to her defeat a greater fortitude than she had ever known before. She rose abruptly and, tightening her coat about her, set off at a firm pace towards her apartment.

When she arrived, Nancy was there, though on the point of leaving for rehearsal, and at once she ran forward and threw her arms around Katharine's neck.

"Darling Katharine," she exclaimed, "I'm so dreadfully sorry." She had seen the special edition, and she quickly went on: "I hope it won't make such a frightful difference. It's the most appalling luck. If only it had happened afterward instead of before!"

Katharine had control of herself now. She said quietly: "Most of the bad luck is on Brandt, when you come to think of it."

"Oh, of course, darling," said Nancy. She paused. "It's like you to look at it that way."

She hung about a moment, anxious to prove her solicitude, fussing a little over Katharine, begging her to sit down, to have a cocktail, a cigarette, to order some dinner right away. But it was plain her concern flowed only from the superficial structure of her mind and that beneath she was pressingly absorbed by her appointment at the theatre, by the progress of rehearsals and all the quick prospect of her own affairs. And she left presently with a little gesture of compunction and affection.

Katharine had no wish for food. She rang for some hot milk, and when it arrived, she drank it with two sleeping tablets. Sleep was the remedy she required. And so, throwing off her clothes, she went immediately to bed.

She did sleep, under the powerful hypnotic, a drowsy, immediate slumber which closed down on her like wings. Yet through that fast embrace thoughts filtered and were transmuted to grotesque and terrorizing dreams.

Her mind, crushed and numb, reverted to that wild illusion which had begun to haunt her and which seemed now to fit the double burden of her sorrow. Mlle de Quercy, the subject of the miniature, came to life, merged into, and became her desolate, unhappy self.

She, Katharine Lorimer, became the living portrait by Holbein, disappointed by life and love, her lips set in that pale perpetual smile, her hand clasping the spray of white carnations, tragic and futile. All the processes of fate by which the miniature had come into her hands at this period of her life seemed predestined and inevitable. A reminder and a presage. It was not the history but the destiny of the unhappy Lucie which repeated itself in her. And that destiny, seen through the phantom shadows of her dream, was enough to make her cry aloud.

She woke with a start, her throat dry, perspiration streaming from her brow, and saw that it was morning. Immediately the realization of her position renewed itself in her unrefreshed and throbbing brain. As if to escape it she jumped out of bed, took a shower, and dressed quickly. A glance into Nancy's room showed her to be still asleep.

Katharine went out. She had no idea of where she was going. Not, of course, to the office. She could not face Breuget, nor the scene of her disaster. Dimly she realized her actions to be pathologic, her mind still half-drugged or wholly stunned. She was in Forty-second Street now, bearing towards Times Square. At the corner she stepped into a drugstore and ordered herself a cup of coffee and a roll. Outside again, she continued through the Square and then, unresistant to the stream of people flowing into the subway entrance, she was borne through the turnstiles and down the steps towards the trains.

Escape! Escape! She was in a train now, which one she knew not, sitting in the crowded compartment, pounding through the subterranean darkness, while the wheels whizzed and shrieked beneath her. She wished only to escape. Terminus. Out again, a windswept platform, with the tang of the sea in her nostrils, the faint sound of breakers in her ears. From the station, into a drab main street full of shuttered shops, oyster bars, sea-food restaurants, shooting galleries, all blistered paint and flaking whitewash, torn billboards and season-old notices. Above and around, gaunt mammoth structures, lifeless and grotesque, the wintry skeletons of an amusement park. A shaft of light struck through the haggard darkness of Katharine's mind and exposed the mad derision of her situation. Her lips twitched with bitter, painful mirth. This place was Coney Island.

It made no difference. Indeed, on the deserted front, with its immense arc of sky and sea, a vast plateau of space cleft by the great liners of the world, the air was cold and clean. Katharine walked miles along the empty boardwalk. She walked all day, back and forth, head bent forward, eyes immobile, as though seeking. But though her head cleared, and the quivering balance of her mind took back its equipoise, she found nothing, nothing but lassitude and despair. The early December darkness drove her back to the lights of the derelict town and thence to the flashing pattern of New York, which received her with crashing mockery, the neon signs vomiting out their colours above the wild inferno of the teeming streets.

As she entered her apartment, plumbing the lowest depths of her desolation, her eye was taken by a pile of white slips, each bearing the habitual printed phrase, "Message awaits you at the office." And at the same moment her telephone rang. It was the house operator.

"Oh, Miss Lorimer," came the pleasant singsong voice, "Mr Breuget has been trying to locate you all afternoon. He's telephoned you half a dozen times and called several times in person."

Only Breuget, thought Katharine sadly, and aloud she said:

"That's all right then, thank you. I'll ring him later."

Apathetically she made to replace the receiver, but before she could disconnect, the operator's voice came back.

"Wait one moment, please, Miss Lorimer. Mr Breuget's on the wire again right now."

A plug clicked in, and Breuget was talking to her.

"Hello! Hello! Is that you, Miss Lorimer? Where in the name of heaven have you been?"

"Her hand pressed against her brow from weariness, Katharine still constrained herself to answer patiently: "I took the day off, Breuget; nothing to be alarmed about at all."

"But, *mon Dieu*," cried Breuget. "Don't you understand what's happened?"

Katharine moistened her lips, beset by the strange hysteric quality of Breuget's tone.

"What's happened?"

"I've been trying to tell you all afternoon," screeched Breuget in perfect paroxysm. "Oh, *mon Dieu!* I cannot hold it any longer, or I'll go up like a balloon. Miss Lorimer, dear Miss Lorimer, we've sold the miniature."

"What!"

"Yes, yes, it's true. Ha, ha! True as the good God above. I want to laugh, I want to sing, I want to dance for joy."

The room spun round about Katharine. She could not believe it. She thought the old man had gone out of his mind. Hurriedly she steadied the receiver at her ear and said in a low, intense voice:

"Breuget! Are you mad?"

He interrupted her wildly. "No, thank God, Miss Lorimer, I'm gloriously sane. Listen, listen! Please listen. Don't interrupt me *please*, or I'll have a stroke. Ascher came in this morning, friendly as a brother. Regretted Brandt's death and all the rest of it. Talked for half an hour. Then came out with the real business. He'd been commissioned to offer us one hundred thousand dollars for the miniature."

Everything was going round again. She gripped the table edge tightly, holding herself erect by a supreme effort of her will. She had to believe Breuget, she had to, there was no avenue of doubt.

"I hope," she gasped weakly, "I hope you accepted?"

"I rather think I did," cried Breuget.

There was a quivering silence, then in a small still voice Katharine whispered: "We've sold it after all—one hundred thousand dollars."

"Yes," shouted Breuget in a frenzy of jubilation. "And the draft's been honoured by the bank. I placed it in at half-past eleven. The money's standing to our credit now. Wait where you are, Miss Lorimer, and I'll come round and tell you everything!"

Katharine dropped back the receiver nervelessly. A quick sobbing breath filled her breast. She swayed towards the couch. Then spinning lights fused suddenly, and everything went dark. For the first time in her life Katharine fainted.

Chapter Sixteen

Next morning was clear and frosty with a high blue sky and a sun which sparkled upon the city. Katharine, her inconceivable emotions of the previous day replaced by a deep and serious sense of thankfulness, sat at the desk in her apartment, writing home. She had already cabled the good news to Walters with instructions to inform the bank, and now, guardedly, she sketched out the turn of events in letters to him and to her mother.

She had barely finished when a knock came upon her door and a radiogram was delivered to her. Tearing it open, she read:

ARRIVING MONDAY EUROPA NANCY'S FIRST NIGHT STOP ROTTEN EXCUSE STOP AM COMING TO TAKE YOU HOME STOP LOVE CHARLEY

So Charley had fulfilled his threat at last! Her smile became warmer yet tinged with a wistful quality as she tucked the slip away. Somehow it pleased her to think of seeing Charley again, he was so indefatigable, so admirable a friend. But, alas, for all his hopes! If she had little enough to offer him before, how much less had she to give him now! And yet she did not know. Charley was a refuge, a kind of safety beacon, always on hand when he was wanted. Was he not the solution to the problem of her love for Madden, the easy answer to all her fears?

She sat for a moment in a reverie which brought the mask of melancholy again upon her face; then, rising, she sealed and stamped her letters and slipped them in the mail chute. Returning, she went and looked out of the window. Though the mark of sadness lingered on her face, the keen crisp beauty of the day was irresistible. And, oh, how grand it was to feel her feet on a sound financial shore again! The miracle, though unbelievable, remained.

Ascher had bought the miniature, not for himself, of course, but for a client. Breuget suspected Joe Shard, the Pittsburgh steel magnate, for whom Ascher usually acted. Shard had been buying Pre-Raphaelite pictures for the new mansion he had built himself, but nothing was likelier than a sudden impulse towards the earlier school. Yet, whoever the purchaser, it made no odds; the money had turned the tide of Katharine's fortunes, and now, deep within herself, she had the firm conviction that never again would they turn back.

The phone rang. "Mr Madden to see you, Miss Lorimer. Shall I send him up?"

Katharine, completely taken by surprise, remained motionless, while the blood drained slowly from her face. Once again that pounding which she knew so well began in her breast and swelled into her throat. "Yes," she managed to say at last. "Send him up."

It was quite logical that he should be here, back in anticipation of Nancy's première, yet the sound of his name even, spoken over the wire, was enough to start that turmoil of emotion which was agony and joy combined.

He came in with unusual directness, yet forgetting for some reason to shake hands. He stood a few paces away from her, his eyes fixed upon her with a queer intentness.

"Nancy's at the theatre," Katharine said. "She's working so hard she's hardly ever here. But I'll ring her for you straight away."

"No, don't," he said quietly. "I'll see Nancy later."

She paused on her way to the telephone. His manner, even more restrained than usual, set a strange, intimidating current vibrating in her breast. Alarmed, she still mustered a smile.

"When did you arrive?"

"I've just got in. Travelled all night from Cleveland." His lips came together, yet his voice was oddly casual. "Katharine, I want to have a word with you, if you don't mind."

Really startled now, she gazed at him with a scrutiny suddenly turned strained. His face, gaunt and shadowed, bore under its impassive mask the stamp of serious distress. His suit was worn with more than his usual carelessness. He had crushed his hat between his hands. All at once a painful thought, already implanted in Katharine's mind, deepened to absolute conviction. She felt instinctively that Madden was in some financial trouble.

Many times she had suspected him of spending more than he could afford. Only the other day she had remonstrated with Nancy on this account. At Graysville he had responsibilities, his mother, the upkeep of the house, and all those needy relations. And now, returning to Cleveland after that long and costly vacation, he had most probably found his business out of gear, paying badly, or perhaps smashed up altogether. No matter how this fixed impression came upon her, come it did, imputing meaning to his manifest anxiety. With her own recent experience fresh in her mind she had a great flow of pity for Chris and with it a tender impulse to help him, to lighten his burden if she could. She took charge of the situation.

"Look here," she said, covering her resolution with a pretence of lightness, "we can't stop indoors on a day like this. If you've nothing better to do, will you lunch with me?"

"Lunch?" he echoed in that same strained tone, as though it were the last thing he expected.

"Yes, lunch," she repeated firmly. "We can talk then. And while we're about it, we'll do it properly. You look horribly tired. A breath of fresh air'll do you good. And Nancy can't possibly be free until four o'clock. I've got an idea. We'll drive up the Hudson to Bear Mountain Inn. With this sun and sky it'll be quite grand."

His face brightened. Again he repeated her words. "Yes, it would be grand." There was a pause which seemed to bring him back temporarily to the mundane. He added: "I'll see about the car."

"No," she answered with decision. "This is my treat. If you think you're going to fling any more money about, you're very much mistaken."

She rang the desk, instructing them to get her a car, and ten minutes later, comfortably wrapped in rugs, they were in the back seat of a long, dark limousine, slipping powerfully through the traffic, and emerging via the George Washington Bridge on the west side of the river. The nearer suburbs dropped quickly behind, and soon they were in the open country racing high up on the left bank of the Hudson. Below them the great river, swollen by snowfalls in the mountains. To their left the hills went tumbling back, clothed in brush and feathered pine, and topped by glittering caps of snow. The air was pure and arctic, the road hard as iron, the whole suffused by a lovely crystal brightness.

How the idea of the drive, almost vetoed by the season of the year, had come to her she scarcely knew. Perhaps an attempt to recapture the Vermont atmosphere. Perhaps instinct had told her how glorious it would be. At any rate, it was impossible not to taste the rapture of the scene, and Katharine turned to Madden with a quick, companionable glance. She tried to make her tone conversational.

"You're not sorry you came?"

Without looking at her he answered: "No! I'm very glad."

She smiled, and remembering, by contrast, her nightmare experience of the day before, she told him something of her wanderings upon the deserted beach and the fortunate termination of that strange adventure.

"So you've sold the miniature," he said, when she concluded. He paused. "Well, I'm mighty pleased about that."

"Yes, I'm in funds now," she answered lightly. "It's just the right moment to ask for an advance."

But her remark, which offered him an opening to discuss his own affairs, passed by unheeded. He remained silent, not attempting even to pursue the conversation, his head sunk a little forward, as though busy with some secret and unalterable thought.

Away ahead of them the cliffs rose with blanker, stonier faces, then parted suddenly, as though pushed by a giant hand, disclosing a prospect of river and undulating valley more magnificent than before. Then they left the riverside, swung to the left along a private road, and, girding the base of Bear Mountain, came to the Inn.

Here the snowfall had been heavier, and on the lower slopes some boys were skiing.

Katharine and Madden got out into the iced wine air, hearing the shouts of the boys, which came cracking down like musket shots. The dry snow on the drive squeaked under their feet. An old porter, in fur cap and mittens, showed them into the hall and up a wide pine staircase, where hung cases of exotic butterflies, a strange reminder on this arctic afternoon of the languid August days. They entered the dining room, a vast half-timbered room built like a hunting lodge, with antlers and the heads of deer upon the walls, and a great half-moon fireplace filled with enormous blazing logs.

Upon her previous visit it had been mid-summer, when tourists and passing motorists had packed the sun-baked room, but though she liked the place then, now Katharine was more powerfully compelled by its deserted rustic splendour. Perhaps because it was already past two o'clock they had the place entirely to themselves and a table set exactly before the gorgeous blaze with a view which compassed the whole striking panorama of the mountains.

The lunch was simple but good: Southern bisque, tenderloin steak, pineapple fritters, and coffee. Yet Madden ate little of it. He continued taciturn, yet attentive to Katharine, his eyes still bent on hers with that dark, inscrutable intensity. Under that gaze Katharine felt a swimming weakness come upon her. Following a longer pause than usual, she said with an attempted smile:

"We came here to talk, didn't we?"

"Yes," he nodded slowly. "At least, as I told you, I have something I must say to you, Katharine."

She dropped her eyes quickly. He spoke her name in such a fashion it made her heart turn over within her. She wanted to help him with all her soul, to make things easy for him at once.

"You're in some trouble," she said hurriedly. "I can see it in your face. But you know I'll do anything I can." She broke off awkwardly. "Tell me, is it money?"

Though his face did not apparently change, a line of perplexity drew between his eyes. He stared at her in a kind of puzzled wonder, then slowly shook his head. "Where did you get that idea, Katharine? I've got all the money I want. Yes, I've got plenty."

The flat indifference of his tone was more convincing than any emphasis. There was no argument, no possibility of doubt. In a flash she saw that she had been mistaken. Why, then, were they here? A tremor went over her. She could not meet his eyes.

He spoke quietly, like a man who states irrevocable fact: "It's more important than that, Katharine, far more important. The plain fact is, Katharine, I'm in love with you."

She sat perfectly still, a wild emotion singing in her blood. They were alone in the room. The warmth of the fire relaxed her body, a sense of exquisite well-being flowed through her limbs.

"I thought I loved Nancy," he went on in that same controlled and level tone. "It was just infatuation. A pretty face after all the years I'd been grinding away at work. Youth and the Mediterranean and all the rest. I fell for it. I didn't know until I met you. But now I do know, Katharine. This is the real thing that comes once in a lifetime. I never knew it could be like this, Katharine. For days I've been fighting it, but it's no use. Even if I can't do anything about it, I've got to tell you. I love you. Yes, Katharine, I love you."

She could not bear it. Wrenching her eyes away from the table, she turned her head aside. "No," she said in a choking voice. "It's not true."

"It is true, Katharine."

"It can't be. It's impossible. How could you—how could you think of such a thing?"

She hardly knew what she was saying. Tears clouded her eyes. Blindly she got up from the table and went towards the window.

"I'm sorry, Katharine. I just had to let you know. I tried to hold out against it, but it wasn't the slightest use."

He rose and followed her, standing in an attitude of entreaty close to her. Outside it had begun to snow. The thin flakes drifted past the window lightly and impalpably as shadows. Beyond those drifting flakes all nature was hushed and motionless. The very trees stood still, like sentinels in sheepskin, posted in glacial immobility. The sky was saffron, and beneath its cupped immensity the earth lay white and glittering. The silence and the beauty of it added to Katharine's hurt. She pressed her hand against her brow. She felt herself overwhelmed and impotent. "Leave me," she whispered. "Please let me be." Again there was silence, crucial and intense. The snow-flakes still fluttered like tiny white birds winging through space.

"I think I see," he said at length in a heavy voice. "It's all on my side. You don't love me?"

It broke the last of her resistance. The pulse in her breast was beating, confusing her beyond thought. A trembling tenderness suffused her. With a little sobbing moan she turned to him.

"Chris! You know I love you with all my soul."

Then she was in his arms, her lips surrendered to his, tears streaming from her eyes. For a moment she clung to him. Unutterable happiness rushed over her. Her heart could not contain it. Then with a cry she tore herself away.

"We can't, Chris. It's impossible! We must think of Nancy."

He was paler now than she. He clasped her hand as though he would never let it go.

"We must think of ourselves. We love each other. That's all that matters."

Reason was coming back to her. Though her whole being was swept and shattered, desperately she fought for self-control.

"It isn't all that matters. Nancy loves you. There's no getting away from that. Never, never, never! You've got a duty to her, and so have I."

He set his teeth, resisting with all his faculties. "But listen, Katharine darling. You love me. You belong to me."

"I will listen, Chris," she answered. "But first you must listen to me. We can't belong to each other. You belong to Nancy. You know how I care for her. I couldn't hurt her. Never! Never! And neither, when you think it, could you."

He did not speak, his face drawn in lines of suffering. He looked into her eyes, which met his steadily, then quickly looked away. Outside against the windowpanes the snow piled softly, relentlessly.

Katharine, with a stifled sob, turned and began to get her things together in preparation for departure. Something final in her actions conquered him. He was close to her, so close the perfume of her hair exhaled to him. He held his breath, then incoherently exclaimed:

"I knew it would be this way, Katharine, from the minute I set out to tell you. But at least it makes it easier to think that you really care for me."

She did not answer, but again looked at him. The grave beauty of her eyes flowed towards him. The sweet anguish of those eyes silenced him. His heart went cold within him. Turning, he followed her from the room.

Chapter Seventeen

The drive back to New York was silent torment. Madden scarcely spoke, but sat rigid in his own corner of the car. Katharine looked straight ahead, her face shadowy and white, her chin pressed into the soft fur of her coat. How she got back to the apartment without completely breaking down, she never understood. But at last they were there, encompassed by the security of lights and people.

It was five o'clock. Nancy had returned from the theatre bringing with her Bertram, Paula Brent, and John Sidney. Cocktails were about, and Nancy, gaily finishing her second, was enraptured at the sight of Madden.

"Hello, honey," she exclaimed loudly and enthusiastically before them all. "I didn't expect you back till tomorrow. It's too lovely. Come and give me a great big hug."

Nancy's mood was one of manifest exhilaration. She did not see Madden's painful hesitation as he stood in the doorway, nor the struggle that showed upon his face. When, with an effort, he went forward, she flung her arms around his neck and pressed her lips against his.

"It's so good to see you, darling," she sighed contentedly. "I've had a beastly day. Bertram is driving us like dogs. This is just what I needed."

Her cheeks were a little flushed and her eyes bright. With her arm still around him, she drew him along beside her and smiled up into his eyes.

There came an imperceptible pause. Katharine's gaze was averted. Her face, still pale, was outwardly composed, but her lips trembled as with pain.

Paula Brent, posed picturesquely in a high chair, glanced queerly from Madden to Katharine.

"Where have you two been? You look all torn up and glacial. As if you'd just come off the mountains."

Katharine felt the others looking at her, too. She stirred. "As a matter of fact," she said detachedly, pulling off her gloves, "we have been in the mountains. We went up the Hudson for lunch. It was wonderful up there in the snow."

"The Hudson!" exclaimed Sidney in a tone of incredulity. He was a flaxen, vapid youth with wavy hair and elegant clothes. His trousers gave him no knees whatever. With an air of supreme wit he added: "Good Lord!"

"No! It sounds interesting to me," murmured Paula politely. "Hope you didn't strike an avalanche. Give me, a cigarette, John."

Katharine coloured imperceptibly. Even Bertram's eyes were on her now. But, with an inner consciousness that nothing could disturb, she went directly towards Nancy and sat beside her.

"Have you had a hard day, my dear?" she asked quietly.

Nancy nodded a trifle exuberantly, waving her empty glass with her free hand. "Simply frightful for all of us. Thank heaven we open Monday. Bertie is driving us like hound dogs. I said that before, didn't I? You know, Oupla! Oupla! Jump through the hoops or you get the whip! But I don't feel so bad now Chris is here. We'll all go out and have a good time. We'll have a lovely time. Have a cocktail, Katharine?"

Katharine refused. After the ice-cold purity of the Bear Mountain air the hot, scented, smoke-laden room made her slightly sick. She observed that Madden was not drinking, either. She turned to Bertram.

"Are you satisfied with the way the show's shaping?"

He laughed, stretching out his legs and contemplating the toes of his shoes with a noncommittal air. "Am I ever satisfied? But I can tell you one thing. That impudent niece of yours is not altogether rotten."

Nancy made a grimace at Bertram.

"Praise from the ringmaster. Oupla! Turn on the radio, someone. After that I think we ought to have some fun."

Young Sidney started the radio, and Nancy, disengaging her arm, threw a swift smile at Madden and began to make up her face, her movements calculating and precise, the colour of her lipstick matching exactly the scarlet enamel of her nails.

It was a lovely, vivid face, Katharine decided, studying Nancy with a new and earnest scrutiny—the eyebrows too thinly pencilled, perhaps, and the lips a little petulant, but the brow clever, the eyes sparkling. And her pose, though studied in its sophistication, struck Katharine as being strangely artless and pathetically young. She shivered slightly. She would never hurt Nancy, never, never, never. Nancy might be spoiled, even selfish, hard, too, and precocious. But she was no more than a child. Sense would come to her, and a deeper sensibility. Marriage to Madden would give her that, and a wider, greater knowledge of the meaning of life.

"What about it, then?" demanded Nancy. "Didn't you all hear me? I want to go places. Let's have dinner at the Rainbow Room and hear those new Tyrolese singers."

Madden's expression remained unreadable. He said with some difficulty: "I don't think I want to go out to-night, Nancy."

Over her shoulder Paula languidly interposed: "The mountaineers are a little tired!"

"Oh, but, honey," protested Nancy with a little pout, "you can't let mama down that way. Mama's sugar baby must be good!"

Even Bertram laughed. Nancy's rapid acquisition of the American idiom was not without its humour. But Madden, staring broodingly at the floor, did not seem amused. A deep and bitter struggle raged within him. At last, however, conscious of Katharine's eyes upon him, he made a gesture of acquiescence. He stood up.

"All right, Nancy," he said. "I'll come."

They all rose, preparing to leave, Nancy taking Madden's arm, Sidney pushing down a last quick drink, Bertram helping Paula with her cloak. But Katharine, firmly pleading a headache, remained behind. She wanted Madden and Nancy to be alone. She prayed that things might straighten themselves out between them during that evening. She prayed it with all her strength.

Chapter Eighteen

On the following morning Katharine had a business appointment on Riverside Drive with a Mrs Van Beuren who was interested, as Breuget had indicated, in their Beauvais tapestry. Actually this tapestry was not Katharine's—it belonged to Richet et Cie, the well-known Paris dealers for whom Katharine was acting as agent—but the commission accruing from a successful sale would most certainly be handsome.

That determination which bulked so largely in her character forced Katharine to carry on as though nothing had occurred. She put on her severest tailored suit and set out for the office at half-past nine. Breuget, looker sprucer and glossier than he had done for weeks, was waiting for her, studying the catalogues of some forthcoming sales. He put them aside as she came in, and jumped up briskly.

"I have the panel packed, Miss Lorimer. We can take it along with us now."

"Good!"

He studied her, smiling, rubbing his hands together gently. "Didn't I say we'd turned the corner? We are going to sell the tapestry. We arc going to do big business this year."

With a quite portentous nod he led the way to the door, where he called a cab and, having solicitously handed Katharine in, he bestowed the precious package beside her and then stepped in himself. They drove off together.

"It's very curious, Miss Lorimer," he remarked, when he had settled himself. "I've been interrogating Ascher all I know, and I can't find out who has bought the miniature."

"Does it matter?" she asked vaguely.

"Oh, it doesn't matter," he agreed with his well-brushed, deprecatory smile. "*Mon dieu*, no! Since we are all right. But it's rather extraordinary none the less. Consider, a work of art of that importance just vanishing off the market— pouff!"

"I thought you said it was for Shard."

"It isn't. No, no! I found that much, out. The good Shard remains faithful to his Pre-Raphaelites."

"Perhaps Ascher still has it?"

"No, Miss Lorimer. He assured me on his oath he'd parted with it to his client."

"Well," Katharine sighed and shook her head, "it's queer, certainly. But we don't have to bother about it. That episode is closed. We've other things to get on with now."

When they reached the house on Riverside Drive, it proved to be a brownstone with tiled window boxes and a fine iron grilled door, evincing that the glory had not all departed from this once famous thoroughfare. Mrs Van Beuren had quite fallen in love with the tapestry, she declared to Katharine, but was undecided as to whether she had a place for it. Already they had too many pictures in the dining room. As for the drawing room upstairs, it was quite unsuitable.

Katharine said little. She followed Mrs Van Beuren over the house, listening in apparent attentiveness. But from the first she had seen that the entrance hall was the ideal situation for the panel. So when they came downstairs again, she inquired:

"Are you satisfied with your hall."

"Why, no," Mrs Van Beuren pecked the air doubtfully. "I've always considered it out of proportion."

"Then suppose you let me do something with it," said Katharine. "Frankly, it could be the nicest feature of this house."

Helped by Breuget and the manservant, she took down a row of rather insignificant prints that hung upon the main wall. In their place she stretched the tapestry, a lovely hunting panel. Below, she moved over an Italian refectory table that had stood, half-hidden, in the morning room. On this she placed two long gesso candlesticks filched from the overcrowded drawing room, and between them a square embossed silver salver.

The transformation was miraculous. The hall took on dignity and character instantly. Even Breuget nodded his approval. As for the little lady of the house, she twittered with excitement.

"Don't move them back," she cried. "Not an inch. I'll have it exactly like that. Exactly!"

"You really want a long mirror on the opposite wall," Katharine suggested, "with a narrow beading and a bevelled glass. We have a really fine George I piece that would suit perfectly."

"Yes, yes," breathed Mrs Van Beuren, "I'll come in and look at it to-morrow."

On their way back again, Breuget turned to Katharine with a respectful chuckle.

"Was I right, Miss Lorimer? The turn of the tide, eh? Don't I feel it in my old bones?"

The turn of the tide! What did it mean to Katharine now? On a pretext she had Breuget drop her at Fifty-seventh Street and made her way on foot towards her hotel. She recollected, as through a mist, that to-day Upton was due and that she ought to meet him on his arrival. But she did not know at what hour the *Europa* would dock.

When she got to the apartment, her first thought was that Charley had already arrived, for on her table stood a long package from the florist's. But immediately she opened the box she knew that she was wrong. There, dazzling her eyes with their beauty, lay a great spray of exquisite white carnations, each perfect, virginal, fragrant. They were from Madden. A pain leaped up in Katharine's heart like a tongue of flame. With eyes half-closed she pressed her cheek against the soft blooms. Their sweetness was more than she could endure. It held for her all the sadness of happiness forsworn. She stood there a long time. Then, opening her eyes, she caught sight of herself unexpectedly in the mirror which hung upon the opposite wall. She was startled by the picture which she made. It was like an evocation of the past, of the miniature, and its meaning in her life. She sighed. "The lady with carnations," she thought sadly. That, henceforth, was her rôle.

No card or message had accompanied the flowers. She knew that Madden would telephone. And indeed almost at once he rang up, his voice low and toneless.

"I'd like to see you, Katharine," he said. "If you can manage, I'd like to see you at once."

Katharine reflected rapidly. Strengthened by the passage of those last few hours, her mind was now unalterably made up. Yet she knew that in reason she must agree to meet him once again, if only to convey the finality of her decision. The time of her weakness was over. Now she could be practical and strong. She would not, however, agree to lunch with him. But casting about in her mind for a meeting place, she chose, with almost melancholy humour, the Metropolitan Museum for their appointment. This, at least, was convenient for both of them, and its formidable galleries would surely dampen the most romantic enterprise.

At a quarter to two she set out for the Metropolitan. The hour had not yet struck when she got there, yet Madden was already awaiting her, pacing up and down in the high entrance hall in full view of the turnstiles. He took her hand silently. But if she expected their interview to take place in that lofty draughty hall, under the frowning and majestic statuary, she was mistaken. He led the way to the far wing where, as it happened, an exhibition of Early American furniture was then being displayed in its original settings. After glancing up and down the quiet gallery he advanced into a pine-panelled room from the coast of Maine. Here he turned and faced her. She saw that he was suffering. His vehemence of yesterday had vanished. He looked worn out. And his voice was strangely uncertain.

"Katharine! I had to see you again. We didn't seem to have a chance to talk things over yesterday. You just make up your mind in a flash. Perhaps you've had time to think differently. Listen, Katharine, we can't get along without each other. Just to see you, it's unbelievable happiness. All night long I've been awake thinking it out. There's only one solution. We must go away together."

Instantly she knew that it was going to be harder, infinitely harder than she had expected, and from the very depths of her being she summoned all her fortitude to meet it.

"Run away," she queried, with a faint semblance of her old smile, "like a couple of children? I don't think so, Chris. We're a little way past that, aren't we?"

"We must do something," he said inarticulately. "We can't ruin both our lives."

With a great effort she made her tone practical and light. "That's exactly what we should do if we went away. We'd be completely wretched and miserable."

"But why, Katharine?"

"Have you forgotten Nancy?"

"I haven't forgotten her. But, oh, that isn't the same thing. She doesn't care that much for me." He went on blindly: "She belongs to a different generation, harder and more selfish. Surely you saw that last night when we came in. Surely you saw it in Vermont. The others did, although they didn't say so. Life falls lighter on her. She'd find it easier to forget."

Katharine shook her head. "She loves you. No, Chris! We can't hurt Nancy. We can't trample over her in a wild scramble for happiness. And it isn't only that. We can't hurt ourselves. If we're different, as you say, if we have deeper loyalties and greater faith, we can't betray them. Don't you see, Chris, it's the one thing, integrity, that's worth keeping? It stands before everything."

"Not before everything!"

Swept away by his emotion, he caught her hand and pressed it against his cheek.

"Don't, Chris, don't," she said instantly.

He released her and stood gripping the edge of the bare oak table, his breath coming quickly, her head averted, as if he could not trust himself to look at her.

"Why do you do that?" she said in that same dull voice. "It only makes things more impossible."

He raised his eyes, suffused with tenderness, and gazed at her.

But again she steeled herself against the wild, dark hunger in his gaze. She must, she must withstand it, or they were lost.

There was a long, a heavy silence, such a silence as had, perhaps, never filled that barren little room in all its early history upon the silent coast of Maine. He stood before her, his cheeks grey, reading her face. Her unwavering eyes convinced him. He stared blankly at the narrow window of the room in which they stood. Minutes passed. At last he spoke.

"Well, then, Katharine. If that's the way you feel about it, there's nothing more to be said. I'll take you back to the apartment right away."

Chapter Nineteen

That same afternoon at half-past three Nancy arrived back at the hotel. She had not expected to leave the theatre until five, for Bertram had called the company for a final drilling preparatory to the evening's opening. Indeed she had told Katharine definitely she would not be home for tea. But the producer, with a characteristic gesture, had suddenly changed his mind and sent them all packing early, with strict injunctions to relax and be on their toes by eight.

Obediently, therefore, Nancy returned to rest, and when the elevator popped her up to the tenth floor, she did not enter the apartment proper but went into her bedroom by the side door with the intention of lying down on her bed. Her entry was quiet, for her mood was abstracted, her mind completely fixed upon the impending performance. And then, suddenly, she heard voices in the sitting room.

At the sound she stood still in the centre of her bedroom. At first her expression was one of surprise. She had not imagined that anyone was in the apartment, and the voices were those of Katharine and Madden. Then gradually her face changed. The voices came to her quite clearly, with chilling and unmistakable distinctness. Madden and Katharine apparently had arrived immediately before her, and now they were saying good-bye. It was a strange good-bye, restrained yet full of sombre meaning, and every word of it struck Nancy like a blow. Still standing motionless, she heard Madden leave the apartment. Five minutes later Katharine went out, too.

A sound broke from Nancy's throat that was half a sob and half a childish ejaculation of dismay. Almost dizzily she entered the living room, now void of everything but the implication of those few words she had overheard. She stared around. How usual its familiar pattern seemed—and yet how different! Chris loved Katharine. Yes, Chris, who was marrying her on Saturday, really loved Katharine. A wave of anger swept over Nancy, then passed, leaving her cold again. She flung herself on the divan, her teeth pressed into her lower lip. She saw it all—Katharine and Madden, their united effort to preserve her happiness. Her pride drew angrily away. She felt herself inadequate and cheap. She had been so sure, so egoistic and complacent. Yes, all her life she had been like that, taking things for granted, giving nothing in return. Now, as if by a lightning revelation, she saw herself, saw exactly where she stood. She burst into frantic tears.

How long she wept she did not know, but at last the storm passed. Quietly she turned on her back, her eyes wearing a look of strangeness, her firm, slender body oddly defenceless. Her thoughts would not move consecutively, yet her capacity for feeling seemed redoubled and intensified. As by a miracle the envelope of childishness was rent from her. She was no longer petty, but mature. The room floated about her. Idly she watched the gradual passage of pale sunlight upon the opposite wall, her mind stopped by recurrent stabs of pain. Within her breast she was conscious, dully, of a slow diffusion, a kind of spiritual regeneration, which spread like the sunlight in the room and gradually brought her warmth.

Finally she sighed deeply and stirred. She looked at the clock—it was nearly five o'clock. Reaching out her arm, she rang calmly for tea. When it came, she drank a cup, then lit a cigarette. A moment later the door opened, and Katharine entered the room.

"Why!" exclaimed Katharine, tipping off her hat and flinging it upon the table. "You're back."

Nancy nodded composedly. "Just got in. Have some tea." How she could speak so calmly she did not know, yet somehow tranquillity was hers.

She poured the tea, listening to Katharine's account of the docking of the *Europa*. Upton, whom Katharine had just left at his hotel, was in the best of good spirits and looking forward tremendously to the show.

There was a silence, then Katharine asked with a faint smile: "Since we're talking of it, how do you feel for tonight?"

Nancy kept her eyes upon the ceiling. "I'm perfectly all right." She paused. "What did you expect?"

Katharine put down her cup. "Oh, I don't know. I thought there might be something I could do for you."

Another pause. Nancy stubbed out her cigarette without turning her head. "I don't have to be fussed over with sherry and biscuits," she remarked with a faintly enigmatic smile. "That belongs back in the crinoline age. Along with stage fright and burnt feathers and floods of tears and fainting attacks." She broke off. "I may do well. I hope so. And that's all there is to it!"

So Katharine had to leave it there. She was, in a sense, surprised at the detachment of Nancy's attitude. She had been prepared for some display of first-night temperament. But Nancy evinced no sign of nervousness. She seemed, indeed, unusually quiet, almost careless of the result.

All that Katharine now considered was Nancy's happiness. For this reason she had no great anticipation of the play's success or failure. That seemed to her of small moment beside the deeper issues now involved. She must attend the première for Nancy's sake, but when it was over, she would effectively remove herself from the tragic scene of her entanglement. Her decision was made. The *Pindaric* sailed on Saturday. Once on board she would close this episode of heartbreaking folly. She had the conviction, sad yet certain, that Nancy and Madden, left to themselves, would solve their difficulties and soon forget her.

Presently Katharine rose to dress. She had arranged to dine early with Upton at Pierre's. Seven o'clock struck, and it was time for her to go. Before she left, she kissed Nancy affectionately and wished her the best of luck. Once again she was puzzled by the blankness of Nancy's mood. "She *is* nervous," thought Katharine with a little compassionate pang, "and she's trying all she can to hide it."

At dinner they were a small party—only Colonel and Mrs Ogden and a Mrs Moran besides Charley and herself. Katharine had insisted she did not want a crowd since she knew that otherwise Charley, who had as many friends in Manhattan as in Mayfair, would have run up his guests to at least a score. Though nothing could remove her gnawing heartache, the dinner, with its immaculate service, its delicate food and wine, and above all its sense of social ease, blunted the edge of her pain. The Ogdens were important people— Colonel Ogden was one of the foremost bankers of New York; and Mrs Moran, thin, dark, and witty, was the wife— or, as she herself satirically declared, the polo widow—of Ralph Moran, Meadowbrook and All American International star. Katharine surmised an old affair between Charley and Mrs Moran which had now reached the nadir of ironic friendship, yet here, in this society, the fact seemed hardly out of place and failed unaccountably to distress her.

Charley was surpassing himself to-night. Creating something of a record, he saw her glass replenished with champagne. Never silent for a moment, his flow of gossip and easy stories kept the table perpetually alive. Towards dessert his smile became a trifle fixed and his utterance a little insecure, but somehow that all seemed part of Charley—generous and harmless and natural. He insisted, following a conference with the wine waiter, upon a bottle of Tokay to follow up the coffee, a rare and—if Charley and the waiter were to be believed—historic vintage from the cellar of the Grand Duke Ferdinand. The rich golden liquor, full of aromatic yet mellow ethers, completed the numbing of Katharine's lacerated sensibilities. As they rose to go, she reflected with a certain bitterness that there were moments in this dreary life when it paid to be pleasantly anaesthetized.

The theatre was almost full when they arrived, and from the crush in the foyer it looked as if it would be packed to suffocation. Bertram, with his cosmopolitan reputation and international connections, had a great following in New York, which assured him—not of a claque, since on more than one occasion the gallery had taken honest exception to his ideas— but at least a first-night audience of critical and expectant friends.

From her seat in the centre orchestra Katharine looked round the house, recognizing many celebrated first-nighters. Then all at once Katharine's eyes fell. At the end of her own row, in a seat near Bertram's own, was Madden. Piercing the haze of the evening, the anguish which struck into her heart was more deadly than angina. The blood left, then rushed towards her brow. Holding her programme with a hand that trembled slightly, she bent her head and made pretence of studying it. He had not seen her. He was with Bertram's party. Where he had dined she did not know, but she knew from Nancy that he was joining her when the show was over.

Here the lights went out, and the conversation died. With a sense of merciful reprieve, Katharine lifted her hot face and fixed her eyes upon the stage, which revealed, without much originality, the interior of the lounge in a house in Sussex. Katharine was already familiar with the play, for she had read the script on the voyage over.

The story was concerned with a middle-aged businessman named Renton, still extravagantly in love with his wife— played by Paula Brent—a languid, rather feline creature given to sentimental amours. At the rise of the curtain she was in the middle of such an affair. Indeed, the first act was given over chiefly to the exposition of her romantic longings and Renton's jealousy.

It was well done, the characterization expert. Yet the audience did not immediately warm to the piece. Perhaps the first scene was played a little slowly. Paula Brent, who took the lead, was first-rate. She was Mrs Renton to the life, fair and languorous, vaguely flabby, and a little past her best, inclined to tea gowns and subdued lighting, burning glances and gentle pressures of the hand. But Paula, in the rôle, was neither new nor startling. She had done the same thing many times. There was polite applause, no more, when the first curtain fell.

"Pretty good," Upton remarked cheerfully. "But we haven't seen Nancy yet."

Mrs Ogden leaned across. "Rather a disadvantage, not being on in the first act."

"I don't know," said her husband thoughtfully. "I'm kind of

waiting for the antidote to that Brent woman. She's awfully good, I guess, but she makes me want to smack her hard."

The second act was set in Renton's office on the following Monday. And here, taking the part of Madge Rogers, Renton's secretary, Nancy came in for the first time. As she made her entry a queer thrill of mingled excitement and pride went through Katharine. She saw instantly that Colonel Ogden was right. The audience was waiting, if not for Nancy, at least for the other woman, the antidote to Mrs Renton, and the possibilities she implied. Moreover, after the first assured line that Nancy so carelessy delivered, Katharine had the conviction that she had never had a better part in her life. She was always good in ultra-modern characterization, but this part seemed made for her. Her nervousness had vanished. She took the personality of the tough, pretty little secretary and burnished it to a sharp hard glitter which almost hurt the eye. Contrasted with the sloppiness of Mrs Renton, her outline had the clean-cut edge of steel.

She was in love with Renton. And when the simple, overworked little man, in an access of wretchedness, revealed the situation at home, she went to work on him deliberately, informing him coolly that his whole attitude was wrong. He was too soft. He ought, she declared, to retaliate in kind by going away for a brief episode with some other woman. Nothing would bring his wife more quickly to her senses. And with the utmost self-possession she offered herself as his companion in the adventure.

"My God," Upton whispered to Katharine, "I'd no idea our little Nancy was as hard-boiled as that."

As the scene developed it was possible to sense the audience sitting up. That slight initial restiveness was gone. Instead, a definite tension filled the house. And again that quick elation took hold of Katharine. She was convinced that all along Nancy had known this to be her chance. And now she was taking it. She was putting it across, she was holding them. She struck the sensibilities of the house with her hard indifference, her passionate yet utterly selfish love for Renton, her burning aim to take everything from life that her beauty and her wits could gather.

Katharine gripped the arms of her seat tightly. She had never seen Nancy act better in her life. Forgetful of herself, her face faintly illumined in the dim auditorium, her lips half-parted, she willed that Nancy might have a great success.

The act finished with Renton's half fascinated, half-bewildered acceptance of the offer, amid a loud burst of applause which continued in increasing waves until Nancy took a curtain by herself. Then a babble of voices broke loose. People stood up, stretching their limbs, yet still excited, and demanding of each other a question which fell thrillingly on Katharine's ear.

"Who is she?" they asked. "Who is she?" It came from every side.

She was Nancy Sherwood, she was Bertram's find. The paragraphs announcing Nancy's arrival on the *Pindaric* were significantly recalled. In the foyer and the lobbies the theme developed, expanded, ran to the limits of exciting conjecture. Bertram himself, his shiny face beaming above his acreage of shirt front, was surrounded by an eager, inquiring crowd. As Katharine passed him on her way back to her seat, he threw an extra smile across his shoulder.

"Didn't I tell you!" he murmured, then added cryptically, "and all due to that one little tooth."

Everyone was back before the second bell buzzed.

"It's so hanged exciting," declared Charley, "you don't have time to finish a cigar."

"Cigar, nothing!" exclaimed Ogden. "I want to know what's going to happen!"

Most of the audience was feeling that way. The general expectation was now intense. The curtain went up in perfect silence. A suite in the Beach Hotel at Littleton-on-Sea, where Renton was now spending the week-end with his secretary. Through the open window just the suggestion of summer, blue skies, and the sea beyond. But Nancy was not on the stage. Four minutes passed while Renton had a vaguely uneasy interview with the hotel manager. A definite restiveness began to develop among the audience. Then Nancy appeared. There was faint applause instantly suppressed. It was clear how completely she had captivated the house.

She wore a beach robe, brightly striped and smart, and in every gesture there was a hint of careless paganism. Lighting a cigarette, she stretched herself at ease on the couch and contemplated, not without satisfaction, her pink lacquered toenails. Then in an offhand voice she informed Renton that his wife was going to divorce him. Renton, though staggered by the remark, clearly felt that she was joking. But she was not joking. All along she had realized that Renton's escapade, far from reconciling his wife to him, would serve actually to afford Mrs Renton grounds for that separation, with full moral and financial honours, which she had long desired. And indeed the next moment Mrs Renton entered.

The scene which followed between the two women, Renton having temporarly collapsed, was one of the highlights of the play, strong, dramatic, and full of suspense. As conceived, in the intention of the author and the original producer, it belonged almost completely to Paula Brent in the character of Mrs Renton. She was, by every rule of logic and the theatre, the dominant, vindictive, triumphant figure. But for once logic did not prevail. Nancy, rising to the occasion through some secret, premeditated design, refused to be subordinated by the leading figure. For every thrust which she received she thrust coolly back. Her lines were not so good as Mrs Renton's, yet she infused them with such icy venom, and winged them with such devilish malice, that they went flying home unerringly. The sense of conflict demanded by the scene was doubled and redoubled by this sudden clash of personalities. The feeling spread to the audience, became almost insupportable.

"My God! The little devil!" whispered someone behind Katharine. "She's stealing the play."

The phrase spread, an undercurrent to the tense surface of emotion. When Paula Brent took her exit, there was scant applause. Every eye remained on Nancy. With the wife out of the way, she was bringing all her influence to bear on the unhappy Renton. The obvious solution, she coolly suggested, was that he should marry her. And going into the bedroom to dress, she left him to digest her ultimatum.

But Renton was at last aware of her hard, deliberate intention.

She had set out to marry him from the first. Standing weakly there, it dawned upon him that he was the victim of those two women—his wife and his mistress. The dilemma was of their making. But he would not accept it. Quickly, on the heels of disillusionment, he pulled a revolver from his pocket and shot himself.

It was meant to be the climax of the play. But now it was not the climax. Nancy entered once again. Bertram had seen to it, of course, had changed the ending of the act with masterly and diabolic cunning. Nancy had heard the shot. She came on slowly, still in her bathrobe, found Renton lying there. She paused, discovered that he was dead. Then followed a moment of acting which capped the first climax and passed it coldly to oblivion.

It was all dumb show on Nancy's part, a slow and piteous pantomime, which touched the topmost pinnacle of art. At the sight of the dead man her cheap effrontery broke. She fell on her knees beside him. Her expression changed; her face, made up and vulgar, was convulsed by an agony of grief. She had loved him. He was dead. Reality struck like an arrow through the brassy sham of her illusions. Blindly she took his hand and pressed it to her lips, an action so tragic, so restrained, it rent the heart of the beholder. Not a word did she speak until, with a gesture of surrender, she dropped the dead man's hand, took up the telephone, and brokenly declared:

"You'd better come on here. A man's just shot himself."

It was terrific. The curtain fell in absolute silence, and for thirty seconds the involuntary tribute of that silence was maintained. The climax of real and unforgettable emotion emerging so unexpectedly from the hard shell of the drama caught the audience by the throat. Many sat speechless. Then the storm of clapping broke, a wild crescendo intermingled with calls for Nancy. It was a riot. And several gentlemen of the press, who gathered up their hats and slid inconspicuously from their seats, knew that it was a riot, or, more fittingly, a wow! There were headlines in this, if they knew anything.

Nancy was taking her curtains now, hand in hand with a palish and rather shadowy Paula Brent, and then alone, bowing with composure to the applause, her arms filled with bouquets. The curtain dropped for the last time. People in the lighted auditorium were talking, gesticulating. There was no question of the sensation. Katharine, lifted out of herself by Nancy's triumph, her heart still torn by that last tragic moment, turned to Upton and the others.

"What do you think of that?" she asked in a throbbing tone. "Wasn't she superb?"

"My Lord!" Charley said, blowing his nose hard. "That had to be seen to be believed. I've never seen Nancy act like that before."

"She's wonderful," cried Mrs Ogden, her eyes moist with tears, "simply wonderful!"

As the audience pressed down the centre aisle Nancy's name was on everyone's lips. And then Katharine became aware of a famous dramatic critic in front of her, wedged in the crowd, conversing in his morose fashion with the critic from a rival paper.

"She's good," Grey was saying. "What d'you think, yourself, Saul?"

"Maybe," Izzard admitted from the corner of his mouth. "Anyhow she's a darned naughty little puss."

"Takin' Brent that way?"

"Sure!"

"Ah! Brent's been askin' for it a long time now, Saul."

"Maybe."

"And this kid's good."

"Yes, Walter," Izzard grunted after due deliberation. "I got a hunch this kid *is* good. Mind you, we've lots of 'em start with a bang and finish up in smoke. But this one won't end in smoke. No, sir. She's got real emotion and sensibility, this one. An' at her age, nowadays, that's corn in Egypt."

The press moved forward, and the two men with it. Yet those thrilling words of Izzard's remained with Katharine. As they turned into the corridor leading towards the stage door they came upon Madden, Bertram, and a crowd of others all going backstage.

As they went through the doorway she glanced at Madden and, in a tone of genuine enthusiasm, exclaimed:

"It was a wonderful performance, wasn't it!"

"Yes, it was marvellous," he answered steadily in a manner which matched her own. "Even Bertram is knocked cold. He says he expected plenty, but nothing like this."

From the undercurrent on his voice and look she drew a sense of definite purpose. A wave of mingled relief and sadness swept over her. She knew he would not go back on his word given her earlier in the day, that his acceptance of the situation, his recognition of his obligations and hers, was irrevocable. Outside the door of Nancy's dressing room they paused, barred momentarily from entering with the rest by the portly figure of Bertram. The benign expression upon Bertram's face indicated that it was quite usual, a mere matter of reaction and a highly strung artistic temperament. For, from within the dressing room, at this, her hour of triumph, there came plainly the passionate sound of Nancy's sobbing.

Chapter Twenty

Next morning Nancy awoke to the unmistakable knowledge of her success. She lay for a few minutes in a dreamy state, breathing the perfume of the flowers which had been brought from the theatre the night before and which now stood in exotic masses about the bedroom. With a strange expression on her little face she mentally reviewed the swift procession of images which memory presented to her.

It bewildered her, almost, to realize that at last the triumph for which she had hoped and fought was hers. Yet she made no attempt at self-deception. She knew instinctively that her performance of the previous night had been better, infinitely better, then anything she had ever done. Perhaps it might even have been great. But she took no credit for her achievement. Before, her vanity would have fed upon this marvellous success, but now she was different. She understood perfectly that everything she had done was the result of her own suffering, of the shock which had torn her adolescent egoism from her and revealed the latent fibre of her soul. Last night she had not acted her part. For the first time in her life she had lived it. And now with a new humility she prayed that she might continue as she had begun.

These thoughts raced swiftly through her mind, then, betraying her inward sensations by no more than a slight constriction of her brow, she sat up slowly, extracted a cigarette from the box on the table beside her bed, and lit it. She smoked it reflectively. Then she rang for breakfast.

The swiftness and obsequiousness of the service, which, though hitherto good, was now a matter of genuflections, gave Nancy, if she had required it, full evidence of her new importance. Two waiters and a chambermaid invaded the room with silent speed as though they had for hours awaited upon a hair trigger her lightest summons. In four minutes the curtains were drawn, the bouquets readjusted, the teacart with its silver, snowy damask, iced fruit juice, steaming coffee, and exquisite brioches was wheeled into position, and Nancy, supported by her pillows, was running through the morning papers.

They were superlative in their notices. Most greeted the play as the best of the season, and all went wild in their acclamation of Nancy.

Almost immediately the telephone began to ring. The first was Bertram—at nine-thirty in the morning, actually Sam Bertram's own fully awake and important voice.

"'Morning, Nancy! Slept well, I hope." The solicitude was paternal, honeyed. There was the suggestion, had it been possible, that Bertie would have cooed. "That's right, that's good, my child. You've seen the morning papers, of course?"

"Yes, Mr Bertram."

"D'you like them, eh?"

"Pretty well, thank you, Mr Bertram," Nancy answered quickly, her eyes fixed upon an imaginary point in space.

"What! Ha! ha! That's a good one! Pull my other leg, will you? Pretty well, thank you! Oh, Lord!" Bertram's laughter boomed richly over the wire. But soon he was serious again. "Now look here, Nancy. You've arrived, and you know it. You've arrived with quite a noticeable bang. Now listen. I'm handling everything. Your part's going to be written up, expanded. I've got to go down to the theatre this morning, but I'll be round to take you out to lunch. But remember one thing. Very special and important. Are you listening with both your little shell-like ears? Good! In case they start bothering you with offers and that sort of thing, don't sign any contracts till you see me. Got that? Sign nothing without consulting me. Good-bye for the present. See you at one o'clock."

That look of queer detachment played around Nancy's lips as

she hung up the receiver, but at a sound outside her door it vanished. By the time Katharine entered she was as bright and collected as ever she had been. She gave back Katharine's good-morning kiss and vivaciously answered her inquiry.

"Yes, of course I slept well, Katharine, darling. What did you expect? Restless agony? Oh, do answer that telephone for me, there's a sweet. It'll keep on all morning—offers of free perfume, face powder, and photographs, all the way down Fifth Avenue."

Katharine lifted the receiver, listened, then covered it with her hand. "It's Madame Lilian of Fifty-Seventh Street," she told Nancy. "You know. . . ."

"I'll say I do," interrupted Nancy briskly. "Give her an appointment, honey—say four this afternoon. Tell her modom, that's me, will be pleased to demonstrate any of her latest confections."

When she had given the message, Katharine sat down upon the edge of the bed and considered Nancy, a spark of amusement showing in her sombre eyes.

"You're a cool customer," she declared at length. "Don't you feel frantically excited?"

Nancy, finishing the last of her fruit juice, shook her head, involving the glass and her own wide eyes fixed on Katharine from above the rim in a rhythmic negation. Her pose of bright sophistication was perfect.

"What's the use? I've had this coming to me for a while, Katharine. It was just the chance I needed. Well, now I've got it. I'm on my way. And believe me, Katharine, I'm not stopping half-way."

"Don't get too confident," Katharine said slowly.

"Darling! Do you want me all shy and bashful? Now don't say any more, but help me push this tray off my bosom, there's a dear. Aren't I nice to own up to a buzzum? And could you possibly make a long arm and shove over my manicure things?"

Obediently Katharine rose and did as she was bid. Though she could not say why, Nancy's attitude perplexed her, with its almost active brilliance. Covertly almost she studied her niece, the small, spare, lovely face with its high cheekbones and sharply cut brows, the thin straight figure stretched in a posture which made her half a boy and half a slim indifferent Amazon.

Again the telephone rang. Unasked, Katharine picked up the instrument. "It's Mr Carl Morris," she said after a moment, "of the Vestris Corporation. He wants an appointment."

Nancy leaned forward. "Morris!" she exclaimed. "Carl Morris of Vestris Films." She bit her lip, always her sign of rapid thought. "When does he want to come?"

"As soon as possible. Now if you like."

"Make it eleven o'clock," said Nancy in an undertone.

The appointment was made. And Nancy, partly relaxed again, began to use her orange stick once more.

"He's terribly important, isn't he?" asked Katharine after a moment.

"Morris!" said Nancy with a little nod of acquiescence. "Yes, he's the biggest man in Hollywood, I suppose. Owns half of Vestris and a dozen other companies besides. He plays about with millions. He is a kind of Hollywood Almighty, Katharine. He's got a little heaven of his own, filled with his own stars, high up for everybody to see, and every now and then he makes a new one and sticks it up among the rest."

Katharine gave her an almost startled scrutiny. There was something new in Nancy's tone, something of satire mingled with good sense, which drew Katharine up abruptly. It was not like Nancy to mock the Hollywood Olympus.

There was a pause. "Well," said Katharine at length, "I've got some shopping to do." She smiled faintly. "I'll leave you to Morris."

A moment later she rose. And in a quarter of an hour she went out of the apartment.

Nancy, however, did not immediately bestir herself and when at half-past ten she rang for the maid, there was no sign of fluster in her preparations. Everything now seemed to go as if pre-arranged and inevitable. She drew a loose dressing gown over her smart pyjama suit, carefully attended to her face and hair, and then, ordering all her flowers to be transferred to the sitting room, she curled herself upon the couch to wait.

She had not long to wait, for Morris arrived exactly on time. He was, in defiance of all those canons which demand that Hollywood directors shall be large, forceful, and loud voiced, a dapper, insignificant man with tiny hands and feet, thin, unruly hair that stood up in moments of excitement like an exiguous coxcomb, and great dark eyes, whose restless timidity immediately betrayed his race.

He came in rapidly, like a man who has a train to catch. Clicking his heels together, continental style, he bowed over Nancy's hand, drew a chair close up to the couch, seated himself, and let his restless gaze go hunting in silence upon her. For quite a time he said nothing, absolutely nothing. Yet what he saw apparently restored him. His nostrils widened to the scent of the roses. He unlimbered himself of an enormous gold case and lit a Turkish cigarette. Then he sat back in his chair with the air of a great artist about to commence the portrait of a lifetime.

"Sharming, sharming," he remarked with a gracious wave of his hand. "I vould like to make a shot of that. Perhaps I vill, eh, Miss Shervoot, for the Vestris Newsreel. Publicity, publicity, *mein Gott*, there's nothing like it." Before she could answer he leaned forward again, re-energized, dynamic. "Now listen to me, Miss Shervoot. I'm a man who comes qvick to the point. Everyvon who knows Carl Morris knows that. You know vy I'm here?"

"I can guess," Nancy answered steadily, her eyes on his.

Morris nodded. "That's goot. Ve begin to understand each other. You've had a great success, eh?"

"Nothing like what I mean to have."

Morris nodded more emphatically. "That's better! Much better! I like to haf ambition mit me ven I get to vork. Now listen, my dear. Ve'll put all the cards on the table. I vos at your show las' night. I like it. I think I am sure, yet I am not qvite sure. I come here this morning. I see for myself. Now I am sure." Impressive pause. "I vont you."

Nancy remained silent, her eyes, impenetrable, fixed on little

Morris, who with an air of immense and intimate significance, bent forward and tapped her with one tiny forefinger upon the knee.

"You know vot I can do, my dear. I can make you a star like Hepburn or like Garbo. I can put you right on the top of the vorld. I chust *do* it. You understand who I am—Carl Morris. I don't talk no stupit nonsense. Ven I make my decision, it is already done. Money makes no difference. I spent von million straight on Anna Herman before got von dime. Now she makes ten millions for me. And plenty more for herself. You seen her last picture? *Mein Gott*, it vas vonderful. Art, drama, passion, every single thing; in the bridal scene alone it cost me thirty thousand dollars for the bed of Emperor Napoleon and no fake about it neither."

He took a quick puff at his cigarette and cast it enthusiastically from him. "Now listen, my dear Miss Shervoot, we are going to come qvickly to be friends. I vont you to come especially to my apartment to-night. Yes, yes, it is all right. I'm too beeg a man not to be on the level. You vill meet my vife and my little Sophie, too. Though I am great artist, I am great family man besides. You otta see my little Sophie. Vell, vell, there's another Shirley Temple if I vont it. You come mit us to-night, my dear. After ve talk and understand each other maybe you'll feel all right about a long-term contract?"

A contract with Morris! Nancy knew exactly what it meant. Morris was right. It, in its own particular sphere, meant the top, the roof, the sky, and nothing less. He would take care of everything, fulfill the most exacting demands: money, publicity, and decisive featuring. Well, she would accept his contract. Hollywood need not interfere with her stage work; that she would most strenuously insist upon. Her eyes wandered distantly, the pupils concentrated, focused to vanishing point. Now indeed she had really done it. At one bound she had soared from obscurity to fame.

They talked for twenty minutes longer, Morris and Nancy, and at the end of it, with a definite understanding established between them, the little man rose, clicked his heels again, and gracefully took his departure.

Only then did Nancy's nonchalance leave her. She sat down

giddily, aware that the comic little man, with his power and his millions, really believed in her and would place her with skilful guidance upon the highest peak of popularity. Suddenly, contained as she was she felt that she was going mad. She pressed her hand against her forehead, tightly, tightly, conquering an ungovernable impulse which she had towards tears.

In the midst of this mood of strange complexity, mingling sorrow and exaltation both, the irrepressible telephone sounded again. Nancy took a step towards it as though she would have cast it into the corner of the room. But this time it was the desk with the information which caused her instantly to pale, that Madden was below.

She stood for a moment, indecisive, her lips quivering. She had not seen him alone since she had overheard him speak to Katharine. And now he was here. She took a deep breath. Determination came back to her.

"Send him up," she said firmly. "And wait!" she added hurriedly. "In a few minutes send up two champagne cocktails."

Her fingers were clenched tightly in her palms. In the short time at her disposal she strove with all her will to capture the right note of inconsequence demanded of her. "If I can act," she thought a little wildly, "please God let me act now."

When Madden appeared, she advanced to meet him, both hands extended gaily towards him.

"I needed just this," she declared, her head thrown back brightly. "You've arrived at the psychological moment. I've had a grand morning, Chris. Congratulate me!"

"On what? A new success?"

She nodded. "Film contract with Morris."

He looked down at her, his face, which now wore an expression of habitual restraint, silently interrogating.

"Yes," she went on. "I've been so busy I haven't even had time to dress. But after all this is quite the proper rig for receiving movie directors. Don't you think it's rather fetching?"

"Sure," he smiled gently. "You know it is. Did Morris fall for it?"

She laughed. "You ought to have seen it. It was better than pantomime. Little four-foot Morris saying his part: 'I vont you, Miss Shervoot. Not in the bed of Napoleon dat cost me thirty thousand dollar. But I vont to make you a star. I vont you to meet Sophie, another Shirley Temple if I vont it. I vont everything, and den I think I vont to go home."

Deliberately she made her impersonation of the little director cruelly to the life. It seemed to send her into fits of mirth. A knock at the door did not disturb her. She stood laughing, while the waiter entered with the champagne cocktails.

"Put them over there," she commanded. "On the table by the couch."

When the waiter had gone, she sat down on the couch. "We didn't have a real chance to see each other last night, Chris. But now we have. And you've got to drink to my success. Now don't look so disapproving. It's quite fitting, I think."

She drank her cocktail quickly while, with greater restraint, he drank his. Outside, the day was grey and overcast. By contrast, the room had an inviting warmth. In the far corner one light cast a soft shaded glow.

"I'm all wound up, Chris," she declared. "I seem calm enough outside. But inside I'm not. And I want you to promise to be nice to me. For I've got something to say you mayn't just care so much about."

He placed his glass upon the table and turned and faced her. He looked rather at a loss. "What do you mean, Nancy?"

There was a short silence.

"I hardly like to tell you."

"Why not?" he said, his voice considerate and full of kindness. "After all, we're being married on Saturday."

Another silence. She moved restively. "It's just that, Chris."

His dark eyes were bent upon her now with a strained compunction.

"Nancy! What on earth are you getting at?"

She took a cigarette, twisted it between her fingers, and lit it. Then she drew a deep inhalation. "I'm sorry, Chris, most terribly sorry. But since it has come to a showdown, we may as well get things straight. I don't want to—in fact, I don't propose to get married for quite a while."

His face had turned grim. He studied her with that same set, strained look, his body rigid, his lips pale. Her sudden declaration had staggered him.

"You promised to marry me on Saturday."

"Yes, I know. But everything's twisted round since last night. My stock's jumped up to the top of the market. I'm going to be tied up with Bertram and Morris—a big Hollywood contract—I haven't time to get married. Besides, it would be fatal publicity for me at the moment." She appeared to relent momentarily. "Oh, don't misunderstand me, Chris. I care for you a lot. But you must see that things are different. When I met you at Nice, I was rather down on my luck. I had a flat spot when I thought I'd never make good. I fell for you terribly, and I sort of felt I wanted taking care of. But now I can take care of myself. Oh, it isn't that I don't want you. You can see that. And I don't want to hurt you. But don't you see it's become a little complicated, a little difficult now?"

"Difficult," echoed Madden with sudden hardness. "You don't know the meaning of the word. Do you mean to say that because you've had this big success you refuse to marry me?"

"Suppose we wait," she temporized.

Madden's eyes were grim. "Wait," he repeated. "You'd have me wait about like a messenger boy. Hang about doing errands for you, carrying your gloves, fetching you flowers, taking you out to lunch when you can spare the time, following you to Hollywood"—his voice rose, not without anger—"playing pet dog to you when you got out of the studios. By God, no, Nancy! I've done it for weeks now, and I don't like it. I didn't ask to be your lap dog. I asked you to marry me."

She was silent. She saw clearly that it was the crisis she had expected, which indeed she had deliberately sought. But nothing,

nothing, was going to stop her now from doing what she had set out to do.

"We were mistaken, Chris," she said slowly. "Let's face it honestly. You'd never have enjoyed my being on the stage."

"I guess you're right," he cried bitterly. "I wanted a wife to be in my home, to. . ."

"Don't say any more," said Nancy quickly. "I don't want to hear it. And in any case it wouldn't be the slightest use."

With effort she cut herself off. She rose abruptly and stood with her back to him, crushing out the end of her cigarette.

He stared at her, his face grey, his spirit suffering and wholly disillusioned. He had been, or at least he had imagined himself, in love with her. He still was fond of her. He was silent a long time. Then, remembering his promise to Katharine, he threw aside his own inclination and tried once more to bridge the gap between them.

"Listen, Nancy," he hazarded. "Have we really lost everything? Isn't there anything we can do to straighten this out?"

She did not stir. "It's no use, Chris," she said in a final voice. "This has been coming to us for a long time. The road I'm going to travel isn't yours. We may be fond of each other, but that makes not the slightest odds. We've got to forget each other. I don't bear you any ill feeling. But once and for all we're through."

There was nothing more to be said. In five minutes he was out of the apartment and heading in the direction of his hotel. He walked mechanically, caught between two extremes of emotion. He had, strangely, no sense of release. But through the heavy burden of his disillusionment came the dismal consciousness that he had failed somehow in his promise, in his obligation to Katharine. In his present mood he could not contemplate the prospect of the future. As for Nancy, though he knew it not, she sat, pale-lipped, in her room, struggling against tears.

Chapter Twenty-One

When Katharine returned to the apartment at half-past five, she sensed immediately that some crisis had occurred. Nancy, who was dressed for the street, had apparently fulfilled her luncheon engagement with Bertram. But though her expression was normal enough, Katharine's intuition told her that something was wrong. She did not speak immediately, however, but first rang for tea. Only when this arrived did she veer towards Nancy and say, between concern and affection:

"Well, tell me? Did the contract fall through?"

Nancy picked up a cigarette and studied it intently. "No, the contract was all right."

"What then?" asked Katharine.

There was a pause. Supported on her elbow, Nancy lit her cigarette and let it come to rest in the corner of her lips. She said deliberately: "In the language of movieland, darling, I've made the greatest sacrifice of my sweet young life."

"Sacrifice!" repeated Katharine in a slightly bewildered tone. "For whom?"

Another pause. Then very distinctly Nancy said: "For my career."

Katharine put down her cup and bent her brows firmly upon Nancy.

"Would you mind telling me just exactly what you mean?"

Under her affectation, Nancy's eyes flinched. But she concealed it. "I've chucked Chris," she answered briefly, "for good."

A silence of stupefaction. The startled quiver that went through Katharine betrayed itself in her face. But following on that emotion came a rush of intolerable feeling so complex and unsettling, so powerfully commingling rage, pity, and downright indignation, that Katharine was really shaken out of herself.

"Nancy!" she cried sharply. "Stop acting and tell me what you've done."

Nancy kept her eyes upon the glowing end of her cigarette. "It's no use getting excited. It's done now. It was either Chris or my career. I had to choose, and of course I couldn't, I couldn't ever, ever, ever give up my career."

"And you've always insisted you could have Chris and your career," protested Katharine.

"Not now," Nancy answered. "Not after last night."

It needed no further explanation. Katharine imagined she saw the whole situation. Immediately everything within her rose in violent protest. Leaning forward she said rapidly, and in quite a different voice:

"You can't do it, Nancy. You're unsettled, perhaps a little above yourself with all the success and flattery you've had. But you can't throw away your happiness like this."

"Who says I'm throwing it away?" replied Nancy evenly.

"I do," Katharine answered earnestly. "And I ought to know."

Nancy sat up and faced Katharine, her face curiously set.

"You don't know. You can't know. I'm the one that's got to make the choice. You can't combine matrimony and art. It's been tried a thousand times before, and it never has worked yet. Oh, I know what I used to say. There's no use going over all that ground again. I've been over it with Chris. Yet I'll go a little bit farther with you, Katharine. This big success makes all the difference. Everything has opened out for me, a wonderful career—success." Her voice turned low and oddly fascinated. "One day I'll be a great actress, a really great actress."

"Don't be too sure," Katharine said flatly. "Others have said the same thing after their first success."

"I'll be different," Nancy answered dreamily. "I'll go on and on. Wait till you see me play Ophelia."

Remembering Izzard's prophetic words, a sense of fatalism came over Katharine. But she put it away from her. She said quickly, pleadingly:

"And even if you do succeed, what is it all going to amount to in the end? Are you going to be happy? Success doesn't mean happiness. Often it means less than nothing. Oh, I know that sounds absurd to you, Nancy; but it's true, most terribly true. I'm older than you, my dear, and I know a little about life. I've had my own experience.

"You talk about your career. Well, I've had my career, made every sacrifice, given up everything that matters for it. And believe me, it isn't, oh, it isn't worth it. If I were starting all over again, I wouldn't give a snap of my fingers for success and all this nonsense about career. I'd rather have a home of my own anywhere, even in the poorest suburbs, and children, and someone to be fond of me in my old age than all the fame and popularity in the world."

Katharine concluded brokenly, swept away by the fervour of her own conviction. But Nancy's expression remained unmoved, a trifle arrogant, even disdainful.

"You may imagine that, Katharine," she said in a hard tone. "But I just won't let myself think that way."

"You'll regret it."

"Oh, no, I won't." Nancy made a slow negation with her head.

There was a throbbing silence. With a strained face Katharine stared at her niece. Hurt and baffled, she still persisted. In a low voice she advanced her final plea.

"But, Nancy, I can't really understand. Don't you love Chris?"

Nancy turned her gaze, now strangely metallic, upon Katharine.

"Yes," she said, "I'm fond of Chris. But perhaps not enough. There's something I want more than Chris. And that's why he had to go."

"I can't believe that," Katharine gasped breathlessly. "At least not of you."

Nancy rose abruptly, her face a pale impenetrable mask. "Sorry you feel that way about it, darling! Tiresome, but it can't be helped. We've got our own lives to lead. And I've decided how I must lead mine. That's all." She glanced at the clock significantly and, pushing back her hair with a quiet gesture, moved towards her bedroom. "Meantime, I've got to get to the theatre by seven."

"Nancy!" Katharine exclaimed in a tone of final entreaty.

But Nancy seemed not to have heard. The door closed behind her with a sharp dramatic click, and at the sound, which somehow symbolized the end of all her striving, Katharine's heart sank, and her figure drooped hopelessly. She had fought with all her strength to convince Nancy, and she had failed. Perhaps she was wrong, yet she saw Nancy as a foolish, precocious child who had thrown her happiness away, and now ran heedlessly along the high edge of disaster, her eyes dazzled by the glitter, her hands outstretched towards the gaudy bubble of illusion.

All at once a shutter seemed to uncover before Katharine's sight. She recollected with a tender pang those early days when Nancy had come to her, a solitary little figure, bereft of her father and her mother, tragic yet strangely tearless. What love she had lavished upon her since then! What plans she had made, and what preparations for her happiness!

A wave of pain passed over Katharine, forcing from her lips a low and bitter sigh. She had torn her heart in two by sending Chris away. She had a strange sensation, unreal yet despairing, that she had lost Chris and Nancy, too. Nothing remained but a weight of blind futility.

Chapter Twenty-Two

It was eight o'clock on Saturday evening, and the floor of Katharine's apartment, littered with tissue paper, coat hangers, rugs, a few articles of clothing, and two half-filled suitcases, presented the melancholy spectacle of a belated packing. Her heavy luggage had gone ahead, and now, having the moment before dismissed the chambermaid, Katharine sat down to rest, her eyes surveying the wreckage of the room, the untidy carpet, empty vases, the choked wastepaper basket, the faded flowers flung upon the window sill. Somehow this litter and confusion seemed to symbolize her own life. Vainly she tried to tell herself that the wreckage would be cleared away, the room restored, refurbished, and renewed. That, alas, would be in preparation for another occupant. It would not be for her.

In three hours' time she would sail on the *Pindaric*, back to England again in the same old ship which had brought her out. Even this struck her as a symptom of the tenor of her life. Upton was returning with her. An hour ago he had gone down to the shipping office, with the facile courtesy which so characterized him, to pick up her ticket and make sure that her cabin arrangements—since she had booked at the last moment—were satisfactory and complete.

Again Katharine admitted Charley's kindness. He was an obliging fellow, a good friend. Yet she knew irrevocably that he could never be more than that to her. Charley was too weak, too facile, far too soft-fibred ever to awaken or to hold her. Her nature demanded someone vital, someone restrained and deep, whose very silences would master her, whose simplicity would evoke the rushing tenderness of her love.

Again she thought of Madden. She loved him with all her heart and soul, such a love as she had never known or ever hoped to know. She would never stop loving him. Already she acknowledged it as her destiny, like that of the poor de Quercy, to carry this secret pain forever in her breast. She thought of him soberly. She had not seen him since the night of the première, yet she knew that he had checked out of his hotel. It did not surprise her that he had not come to her. At first, perhaps, she had expected him. But now she saw the situation as too confused and too upsetting for such a simple ending. The human emotions were delicately attuned. Nancy's behaviour must have hurt him badly, altered his outlook, shifted his sense of values.

She felt convinced that he had returned to Cleveland, sick of the vagaries of women, disillusioned and equally determined to close the painful chapter of his recent experience. She was aware of the telephone at her elbow, an instrument which might have been created to restore communication between Madden and herself, yet she would have died sooner than avail herself of it. Her pride forbade it, and the bitter memory of that moment in the Metropolitan when she had thrown her happiness away. No, no! Let him keep away from her if he did not wish to come. That was the best solution, the clean-cut remedy. It offered the easiest outlet of escape.

Presently he would forget her, marry some American girl, young and beautiful, who would make him happy. She winced, remembering with a little pang that early trivial episode in her life. At least George Cooper had not mourned her long, and it was a precedent which Madden might well follow. She would remain unwanted and unlamented, following the orbit of her lonely star.

She got up slowly, began to toss the last few articles into her travelling case. Nancy had already left for the theatre and would probably not be free until after the time of sailing. Thinking of Nancy, Katharine sighed. She seemed so different now, so elusive and remote. She would not talk of Madden or of her own affairs.

Her whole life seemed bound, as though consecrated, to the service of the stage.

Nancy's success continued, blazed in bright lights across the sky, and was now in fact assured. Apparently she had not sacrificed Madden in vain. The contract with Morris was signed. She was going to Hollywood in the spring at a salary which must have satisfied the most exorbitant demand. Moreover, despite her allegiance to Morris, she was still on the best of terms with Bertram, having arranged that he should handle the theatrical side of her work. He had altered the structure of the play, amplifying her part, giving her extra and more telling lines. He was full of enthusiasm and plans. Nancy was to lead, for certain, in his next production. He had given a special press interview under the heading, "A New Star Rises", which dealt exclusively with Nancy and his own unerring faculty for discovering genius.

Katharine snapped the cases shut with a kind of melancholy finality. It was finished now. Nothing remained but to ring the office, give her instructions to the porter, and silently depart. It was very quiet in the bedroom, and extraordinarily still. Softly, from a neighbouring apartment across the corridor, the muted sound of a radio came stealing in, an almost ghostly music, familiar yet curiously remote. Instinctively Katharine listened, then with a shiver of pain recollection came to her. It was the refrain to which she and Madden had danced upon the *Pindaric*. Silly words and sentimental music. Yet scalding tears filled Katharine's eyes. She dashed them away. Courage! That was all remaining to her now. Yet the melody held her, played upon her heartstrings with haunting, desperate insistence.

She put on her hat, threw on her coat. She took a last look round the bedroom and made to wrench herself away. Her limbs were heavy, her head light. She walked into her sitting room. And there, just inside the doorway, was Madden.

Her heart stood still within her, then raced with quivering life. So unexpected was the sight of him, so painfully and suddenly disturbing, she felt it as a trick of vision or perhaps some wild illusion of her fancy. But it was he. And with a grave composure that made her own agitation seem pitiful and absurd he advanced towards her.

"I couldn't let you go," he said in a tone of quiet friendliness, "without coming to say good-bye."

So it was that! He had come merely to say good-bye. Her throbbing pulses stilled again, and upon her there settled a white, unnatural rigidity.

"After all," he went on more lightly, "we agreed a long time ago we must be friends. And now we want to part good friends."

Her face was stiff and pale. Yet she saw that some answer was demanded of her. "Yes, we must part as friends," she managed to say.

"That's right." He glanced about the room with unusual briskness and demanded: "Where's Upton?"

"Gone down to the ship," she answered blindly.

"Ah! That's a pity. I wanted to say good-bye to him, too."

Head averted, eyes still upon the floor, she flushed slightly. His aggressive cheerfulness, never apparent to her before, bludgeoned her. Yet, because she suffered, her pride rose to support her.

"I'll give him your message," she said quietly.

"Thanks, Katharine." He paused, rubbing his hands together with that incredible alacrity, like a boy on Christmas morning. "He's a lucky fellow, travelling back with you like this."

"I'm glad you think so."

The words, into which she struggled to infuse a carelessness matching his own, stifled her. There was a hollow silence. She felt that if she did not terminate the interview, she would die. Dumbly she raised her head and forced herself to look at him.

"I'm going now," she declared. "I don't think we have anything more to say."

He interposed. "Please! Just one thing." He had seated himself casually upon the edge of the table, and now, with a show of indifference, from the outside pocket of his overcoat he produced a paper parcel. "Besides saying good-bye I want to give you a little keepsake."

She stared at him with suffering, wounded eyes, snared by the pitfall of her own contrivance. Mechanically she accepted the small package he held out to her. Under her stiff fingers the untidy wrapping and loosely knotted string fell away. Then a sort of vertigo possessed her. Giddily she contemplated the familiar green case. With a cry she opened it. Inside reposed the Holbein miniature.

"You!" she gasped at last. "It was you who bought it."

"Why not?" He answered easily. "It's one of the little things I can well afford."

She simply could not speak. In a daze of flashing light she perceived that his intention had saved her from disaster. Upon the news of Brandt's death he had acted instantly though Ascher. But how? Bewildered, her poor mind groping between the fact and all her earlier suppositions could not cope with it. She trembled upon the brink of tears.

He shook his head. "You got me wrong, didn't you, Katharine? In London and 'way up in Vermont, too. But I'm not a poor man. I'm rich, so rich I don't have to bother to look it. It isn't a little outfit I belong with. That's how I began, but I guess I've worked it up some in these last ten years. I fixed the last amalgamation before I sailed for Europe. Now, if it interests you, Katharine, I'm president of International Adhesives."

She stared at him, stunned. The name he mentioned devastated her. It was a mammoth corporation, a foundation of international solidity and fame. Its posters blazoned the countryside from coast to coast. It was universal. It made everything that sticks, from paper paste to adhesive plaster. Its debentures and preference holdings were a gilt-edged quotation on Wall Street, in London, on the Bourse. Vaguely she remembered seeing photographs of the giant plant in some magazine—the acres of factory buildings, the foundries, tanyards, shops and packing houses, the canteens, the restrooms for employees, the playing fields, gymnasium, and swimming pool. And he, Madden, whom she had fancied poor, was its head, the sole controller of its power. It was too much for her suffering, baffled comprehension.

"I must go," she whispered. "It's time. Charley will be waiting."

Unseeingly, her head lowered, she placed the miniature upon the table and started towards the door.

But quickly he came forward, intercepting her. His manner was quite changed. All his earlier levity was gone, his casual inconsequence fallen from him like a mask. Now there dawned upon his face a great tenderness, and in his dark eyes a look which strangely illumined them.

"Upton isn't waiting," he said steadily. "He's going on to Florida by the night plane. But he's booked two passages on the boat sure enough. Your passage, Katharine. And mine."

She gave a little anguished cry. "Chris!"

Gazing deeply into her eyes, he said slowly: "Did you think I would really let you go? After Nancy had done everything to bring us both together?"

She gazed at him blindly. "I don't understand."

"Listen, Katharine," he went on, even more slowly. "Nancy knew that we were in love with each other. She discovered it just before the première. And then she suddenly grew up. All the real fineness of her character came out. She did what she thought best, and in the way she knew to be the best."

Katharine saw everything in a flash. "Nancy," she whispered.

He nodded his head. "It was Bertram put me wise to what had happened, and then I tumbled to it all myself. He says it's been the making of Nancy. She'll go ahead now, right to the very top of the tree. She'll play Ophelia, sure enough. As for us—well, we're not going to let her down."

Her vision was blurred by tears, her heart strained in her breast as though unable to sustain the emotion which filled it. Then she was in his arms. He held her close to him, feeling those wild heartbeats against his own, soothing her.

"Yes, you're going to marry me all right," he murmured gently. "In your little old church, Katharine, just round the corner from the old Inn Yard. That's where I first fell in love with you, though I didn't realize it at the time. We'll stop a bit in London, settle up that old business of yours for good, then take the jump back to Vermont. I know some folks that'll be mighty glad to see you there.

After that maybe you wouldn't mind dropping in on Cleveland. There's a pretty fine site there, Katharine. Right up on the hill. I guess we could build a home there we might be happy in."

She did not speak. Her heart was too full for speech. She pressed her cheek against his coat. And then her eye caught the miniature which lay in its still open case upon the table. Another wave of happiness mingled with relief rushed over her. How had the mad illusion ever possessed her that her destiny was bound by sadness to the miniature! It was bound by joy alone. That other was only a fantasy of her own foreboding. It was over now—a nightmare that would never come true. Loneliness would not be her portion after all. The eyes of Lucie met her without sadness, without rancour, smiling.

Two hours later they stood upon the top deck of the *Pindaric* watching the slow recession of the spangled squares and rectangles, the glittering sky pattern of New York. It was a night of velvet, soft and darkly luminous, filled with the play of water and the quiet pulsing of the engines. A white moon shed a soft radiance over them and made a long straight pathway upon the waters down which the ship, bearing them, seemed silently to pass. They stood together at the rail. Madden had linked her closely to him with his arm. There was no need for words. But suddenly they were conscious of a steward's approaching them. Madden turned.

"What's the matter?" he asked.

The man answered: "I had instructions to deliver this personally, sir."

Madden snapped the cord and opened the box. Then he handed it to Katharine in silence.

The little spray of white carnations was lustrous in the moonlight. And the card said simply:

"Be happy, both of you—Nancy."

Printed in Great Britain
by Amazon